Sacrificial Maiden

On the flat altar where the god Mizran had been worshiped long ago lay the white body of a naked girl. Golden chains held her wrists, golden links her ankles. . . .

She was petrified with fright—or drugs. . . .

"Thy blood accepts her, dark Pult-hoom!" droned the priest. . . .

Kothar stepped forward. . . .

"Blasphemer!" screeched the priest.

He drew back the bowl to hurl it.

Kothar leaped. The horn bow went out, hit the bowl, tilting it as horn rang against silver. That dread fluid gushed from the bowl, splattered across the face and throat of the high priest.

His scream was shrill, agonized.

KOTHAR OF THE MAGIC SWORD!

by Gardner F. Fox

BELMONT BOOKS • NEW YORK CITY

KOTHAR OF THE MAGIC SWORD
A BELMONT BOOK—SEPTEMBER 1969

Published by
Belmont Productions, Inc.
185 Madison Avenue, New York, N.Y. 10016

PRINTED IN THE UNITED STATES OF AMERICA

KOTHAR OF
THE MAGIC SWORD

Foreword --- 5

The Helix From Beyond ----------------- 9

A Plague of Demons ----------------------73

FOREWORD

These are tales of Kothar, barbarian swordsman, and of the blade Frostfire, the sword given to him by Afgorkon, the living-dead wizard. His world is a dying one, for the planet upon which he lives, in the pagan splendor of a land sinking toward oblivion, is hurtling back upon its beginnings. The entire universe is collapsing now, instead of expanding.

In his world are to be found wizards, witches, warlocks and much magic, as well as the clash of swords that can withstand spells and cantraips, together with the mighty men who hold them. Across that land, from the ice wastes of Thuum to the desert lands of Oasia and beyond, he stands like a colossus, brave to the point of foolhardiness, a thief when his belly is empty enough to demand he satisfy it, a maker and an unmaker of kings and queens, a brash lover of women, a warrior when it suits his needs.

Above all else, he is an adventurer.

To see a new temple on the horizon (which may hold treasure to loot), to kiss new lips (since he admires pretty new female faces and the bodies below them), to ride where death beckons and a maytime happiness waits, Kothar will risk much. While it is true that, because he carries Frostfire, he can never be otherwise

5

wealthy, it is also true that he never quite gives up his ambitions to be rich.

Locked behind the bars of a silver cage hung on chains high up in the palace of Queen Elfa of Commoral hangs the witch-woman Red Lori, beautiful and deadly, who yearns to punish Kothar for having hung her there, yet can think of no vengeance satisfactory to her feminine fury. And so her green eyes brood on Kothar as he travels across his world, and sometimes she reaches down to touch him, to remind him he is human and belongs to her for her punishing. Upon occasion, it pleases her to travel with him, in spirit, and even, at times, in body.

For, since she thinks of Kothar as her property, belonging to her for her revenge, she wishes nothing to happen to him until she herself is ready to determine and execute that vengeance. There are times when she will lead him into danger, into the clutches of a human monster or a demon out of some forgotten Hell, just to tantalize him, to see if he is worthy of her hatred.

And so, battling men and succubi, snarling and savage, equipped only with his wit, his brawn and his magic sword Frostfire, Kothar strides like an elemental through the lands of his world. Those lands teem with wizardry, with greeds and hates, with men eager to pit their strengths against his own, with women who sense the pagan deviltry in this giant of a man with the golden mane and find themselves attracted to it.

My sociological and archeological friends assure me that man himself can sink to such savagery, such primitive ways of life, in the last years of his existence. Crude civilization will rise and fall in mimickry of those which have gone before and now lie as dust on the planets of the universe. In short, man suffers a

second childhood, when things known at the very beginnings, are known at the end.

Frostfire in hand, Kothar strides across this segment
out of Time. . . .

THE HELIX FROM BEYOND

1

Two men swam steadily through the cold waters of Lake Lotusine.

One man was small, with the dark skin and curly black hair of the true southlander. He was naked except for a white loincloth about his middle and a belt that held his curved knife. He swam without strain; he was part water-rat, Rufflod liked to boast in the waterfront taverns. He was on his way to steal the greatest treasure in his world, and so he swam through the lake waters as he had never swum before.

The man who moved beside him, great muscles rolling under a sun-bronzed hide, was almost twice the size of Rufflod. No southerner, he: his long yellow hair floated in the water when it was not plastered to the face he thrust out of the rippling waters at his every second stroke. His was the fair skin of the northern man, the yellow hair, the blue eyes and muscular bulk.

"Where away, Rufflod?" the big man growled.

"Not far, not far," the other called softly.

"By Dwallka! If you've lured me on a fool's errand, I'll use that khanjar you carry to flay the skin from your bones!"

"Just beyond the point—look!"

Kothar wallowed in the slight waves. Ah, he could see it now, like a golden nimbus beyond the trees and the few buildings there on the point of land jutting out

9

from the warehouses lining this corner of the city of
Romm. There was a glow in the night, low down
beyond the trees silhouetted against that yellow radiance. Beams of lanthorn-light shafted upward toward
the stars. With it came the sound of harps and flutes,
where the emperor Kyros made revel in his golden
galley.

Kothar had never seen Kyros, emperor of Avalonia,
though rumors of the fat, half-demented little man had
crept across the Roof of the World and the Haunted
Regions into the land of the baron lords, where he had
been employed for a little while as a mercenary. Thinking of the wealth of Avalonia, of the green emerald
rings worth kingdoms, each of them, of the pale emerald eyeglass through which the emperor looked at the
world about him, tempted the juices of cupidity which
lay close to the surface of the barbarian swordsman.

I will go into Avalonia and see this Kyros emperor,
he had told himself over a campfire on the edge of the
Unknown Land. And if by chance his emerald eyeglass
or one of his emerald rings falls into my hand during
my visit, I will use it to buy a little castle and a few
acres of land around Grondel Bay, which is my homeland.

He had been in the great city of Romm, where
Emperor Kyros held court, for close to three weeks. His
purse had shrunk steadily in those days, he had never
been much of a money-grubber; and when he ate,
Kothar feasted like a northern troll in his cave-home,
gluttonously and against the bite of coming winter
winds. It was over a haunch of venison and a goblet of
chilled Salernian wine that Rufflod had sighted him.

The little thief had been hunting for a partner. He
was sly of wit and mind, and his body was tough as
rawhide, but he needed more muscles for the job he
had in mind than his arms and legs possessed. To his

hot dark eyes, where they peered from the shadow of a leather curtain on the feasting barbarian at the Inn of the Seven Furies, the Cumberian looked like the man he had pictured in his mind.

They had struck their bargain quickly enough. Rufflod was a convincing talker, and he was free with the silver pieces in his purse.

"Come with me to the home of the merchant Nestorius," Rufflod invited. "He is a wealthy man, he furnished this silver as a handfast of his good will. He will tell you what he wants us to steal from Kyros."

Kothar pulled his sword Frostfire around from his side so it stood up tall and magnificent between his thickly thewed legs, bare under his fur kilt. The sword was a gift from the dead magician Afgorkon, given him when he had come staggering and bloody off the field of battle at the Plain of Dead Trees to fall by sheer accident into the crypt which had sheltered the lych Afgorkon for fifty thousand years.

The sword was the only wealth he owned, the only wealth—according to the words of Afgorkon—that he could ever own, so long as it hung by his side. To Kothar, Frostfire was riches enough, though he hungered at times for a bit of gold or a jewel or two with which to buy a particularly attractive wench's favors.

"What has Nestorius to do with this treasure?" he growled.

"Sssst! Not so loud. It was Nestorius who told Thaladomis the magician where he might sell it—to the emperor. Thaladomis did not give Nestorius his commission."

Kothar grinned, showing even white teeth in his handsome face, topped by a mane of shaggy yellow hair. His blue eyes burned in his skin like balls of cobalt. "So Thaladomis cheated him, did he? Well, that's the way of magicians."

Rufflod grinned. He liked this big man in the mail shirt and the fur tunic, with his wide shoulders and long arms rippling with heavy muscles. The size and apparent strength of Kothar made Rufflod shiver, however, whenever he looked into those blue eyes, hard as northland ice and cold as the wind called Borean.

"Now Nestorius wants his own back, and hires us to get it for him."

The barbarian frowned. "What is this helix?"

Rufflod shrugged. "I don't know. It does—strange things, things that terrify me, if what Nestorius has whispered to me be true. However, if you like, he can tell you that himself. Come along."

They went by way of the cobblestoned streets of ancient Romm, past wine shops and taverns where naked women danced to entice customers to buy their favors. They shouldered past little knots of men in heavy all-purpose cloaks who lingered in the shadows assessing each passer-by with eyes that took in wealth, extent of drunkenness and ability to fight back, all at one raking glance. Romm in the torchlights of its nights was no place for the weak of spirit or body.

The merchant Nestorius lived on the edge of the great palaces of the Romm nobility. His town house was set flush to the street, and extended for almost an entire block with a high wall about its gardens, where a woman made sweet music on a flute beneath a flowering tree. Rufflod knocked, the music halted. There was the sound of slippered feet running on garden paving-stones.

"Who's there? This is Crylla, slavegirl to Nestorius."

"Rufflod here—with a friend to see the great merchant."

An iron latch clicked. A bolt was drawn back.

A pretty face set with hanging brown hair, with eyes made brilliant by the rich green kohl tints of distant

Sysyphea and a red mouth that made Kothar think of kisses, peered out at them. She frowned at Rufflod, but dimpled a smile at the barbarian where he towered in the background.

"He's been expecting you. You're late." She swung the door wide, so that the men could step into the garden. There was a sweetness in the air, suddenly, making the Cumberian wonder if it were the girl or the flowering shrubs and trees behind her.

"It wasn't easy to find him," Rufflod jerked a thumb at Kothar. The girl flirted with the barbarian, lowering and raising her lashes, smiling breathlessly as her bold eyes raked his muscular bulk.

"He's a big one, all right," she admitted.

"Just the man to help me in the job," Rufflod nodded.

The merchant Nestorius agreed with his hireling, for he beamed on Kothar like a father welcoming a rich prodigal in an upper chamber that was his study. He was a tall, lean man with a saturnine face out of which wise eyes studied his world for its taking. Clad in a brocaded garment trimmed in fur, he stood beside a long table on which were spread parchment maps of the lands of Avalonia, Aegypton, Vandacia and Oasia to the south, the unexplored lands and the vast steppes of Mongrolia to the east, Commoral to the north. To far-distant lands went the caravans and safaris of Nestorius, and his finger moved along those maps with every horse, every camel, every hired mercenary and trader in his employ.

"You made a good choice, Rufflod. This one looks like a fighter." To Kothar he said, "I assume you can fight?"

The barbarian merely growled in his throat. "What do I get out of the venture—except bruises and cuts?"

Nestorius chuckled, turning to a shelf behind him

where a number of fat leather purses stood. "This," he murmured, and tossed a bag to Kothar.

The Cumberian pulled the purse-strings. Out of the almoner tumbled a dozen big jewels, tiny bars of solid gold, a few coins of Romm. He blinked. By Dwallka! This was a fortune to make a man mad. For an instant he was tempted between the wealth in his palm and his ownership of Frostfire, but only for the moment.

Secretly, he wondered if he would be able to keep this hoard, or if the spell on Frostfire, cast there by Afgorkon, would compel him to lose it, in one manner or another. His big shoulders moved restlessly. Let the Fates send their wills, he would walk his road as he saw fit.

"I'll go," he nodded, placing the jewels and the little gold bars back inside the leather bag. "For this much wealth—ask for the emperor or his emerald eyeglass or this thing called a helix, and I'll bring them to you."

"Boaster," snorted Rufflod.

But Nestorius nodded gravely. "Aye, I think you will—if it's possible. You speak the word 'helix' as if you think it nothing but a toy to please an old man's whim, as compared to the emerald eyeglass or the rings that Kyros wears. Well, think what you will, if you bring it back to me, I'll demonstrate for you what the helix can do in the hands of a man wise enough to know its use."

Kothar placed the almoner on the tabletop, beside the map. Nestorius raised his eyebrows questioningly. The barbarian said, "I wouldn't want to lose my fee during a fight. It's safer here. When we bring you the helix, I'll take the purse."

The merchant nodded approvingly. "It will be safe."

Now as he swam toward the great golden galley of the emperor, Kothar thought about his purse and the pleasures it would bring him. He did not think the water cold, he had spent his boyhood bathing in waters far icier than these southern lakes, in Grondel Bay. He was as a seal in water, huge and frolicking and utterly without fear, appearing to slither rather than swim, whereas Rufflod, for all his water-rat ability, seemed to labor ever so slightly.

They were out beyond the Point.

They could see the galley clearly, huge and massive, with its fore and aft bulwarks like walls of solid gold. At the prow a magnificent swan's head towered upward, beak half-open as if sending out its trumpeting call to battle, while at the stern, a smaller head upon a smaller neck seemed to rest as if asleep. Between one head and the other, a covered deck held two banks of oars, worked by galley slaves close to the waterline. The oars were red, gilded at their blades, and they hung motionless now while the nobles of Romm made sport with their women and their emperor on the gilded deck planks.

Kothar could see nothing of the deck itself, his attention was fastened on the aft section of the ship, where the bulwarks dipped in a half-circle toward the water. The golden galley had been built to drift on Lake Lotusine, it had never been shaped to toil in the waters of the great Salt Sea where the storms were gusty and terrible; the royal triremes were made for that, and for defending the coastline.

His eyes, as he swam, went often to the pale lights visible in the golden stern. There was a cabin there, well-lighted, and by the reflection of those oil lamps he could make out the corrugations in the hull of the galley, where it swelled like the breast of the swan it imitated. Those indentations that resembled swan's feathers might give him the handholds he needed to reach that cabin.

Rufflod had told him the emperor kept the helix in

the after cabin, illumined by votive lamps and with guards posted outside the bolted cabin door. "It will not be easy," he had muttered, shucking out of his clothes near a great piling from the quay, just before they had begun their swim. "Kyros guards the helix better than he does his empress."

Kothar knew what the thief meant, now. The rails were lined with soldiers in the gilded helmets and cuirasses of the Prokorian Guard. Tough men, specially selected for their fighting abilities, all of them.

He began to understand why Nestorius had wanted him along as a bodyguard to Rufflod. Those javelins glinting in the torchlight looked very deadly; so did the short swords hanging in the gilded scabbards close to the brawny hands of the guardsmen. Around his neck on his swordbelt, Frostfire made a good weight. Though the great blade dragged on him slightly, like an anchor, it was a reassuring thing to know it was there within his own finger-reach.

They were nearer to the galley, now.

Rufflod moved closer. "Fetch!" he breathed, and dove.

Kothar was after him in a moment, his brown skin glistening with water where moonlight touched it, shaking his yellow mane and making the water drops fly an instant before he too disappeared in the murky dark waters. Underwater, his huge lungs filled with air, he was a shadow slipping past the little thief.

His outstretched hand felt cold metal beneath the surface. Kothar came up silently, poking his head out like a curious otter. His fingers went over the gold feathers fitted into place on the rounded stern.

Rufflod said, out of the darkness, "Can you climb that?"

The barbarian snorted.

Rufflod grinned, "All right, I only asked. We must

mount to the after figurehead, to the swan's beak. It is the only place where curious eyes will not be able to see us. Here, let me go first to—"

He spoke to empty air. Like a cat, the Cumberian was swarming up that round bow, fingers and bare toes clinging like limpets to the golden feathers. He moved upward with graceful ease; Kothar had climbed the great glacier of Thuum as a boy and young man, and the muscles in his mighty back tautened and loosed to his every few feet of progress.

Rufflod grunted and went after him.

Naked but for the wet cloth at his loins, the sword Frostfire in its belt and scabbard about his neck, Kothar clung to the swan's head. Below and behind him he could hear the thrumming of the harps, the wild piping of the flutes. Turning his head slightly he found he could scan the galley deck, where fat Kyros was perched on a small ivory throne over which had been flung half a dozen leopard pelts.

Sipping from a golden goblet, Kyros watched an almost-naked Oasian temple girl swing her dusky hips and shake her shoulders, stamping with bare feet on the gilded deck planks as she performed a lewd dance common in the temples of her southland. The emperor, as well as every other man and woman on the deck, could not have torn his eyes from the smooth flesh of the lithe, lovely dancing girl.

No one was thinking about the after cabin.

Rufflod pulled himself up beside him.

"I've got to get inside the cabin. Can you support me while I do, holding my ankle, and letting me get a look inside?"

"Can I hold a sack of meal?"

Rufflod nodded, content, putting his head down first and sliding over the beak, letting his palms rest on the golden feathers for support. Kothar put a huge hand over the slim ankle and gripped it. He crawled along the swan's head, letting Rufflod down more and more, so that he dangled here, fumbling at the open cabin windows.

"I see it," Rufflod muttered. "Gods—how magnificent!"

The little man was even with the window, gripping the sill, tightening his fingers ready to kick free of the barbarian. His voice came oddly muffled as he murmured, "Let me go, let go!"

Kothar opened his fingers.

Like an agile monkey, the small man dropped, catching his weight with his fingerhold on the sill and hitting the gold stern with his bare toes in a silent jar. Then he was pulling himself upward and bobbling in through the window.

Kothar lay quiet as a hunting tiger, listening. He could hear no sound from below him, no voice of an aroused guardsman, no warning bell clanging in the night. His barbarian instincts were up and flaring, for Rufflod should be at the window, lifting out the helix so that Kothar might grasp it and fasten it to his swordbelt.

By Dwallka! Where was the man?

What was happening below him in that cabin lighted by the pallid glow? There were no guards in there, they would have shouted the alarm, their swords would have made metallic sounds coming out of their scabbards as they hurled themselves on Rufflod.

Only an eerie silence in the darkness greeted his straining ears. Like a snake and as quietly, the Cumberian shifted position.

He was just beginning to slide downward to have a look for himself when the scream erupted in the cabin. It hung a moment in the air, filled with terror, full of that dread of the unknown gulfs of time and space that effect every human being. . . .

"Aiiiigghh-ahhhhh!"

The music and the singing stopped on the deck. The emperor lifted his head, forgetting the Oasian and his wine goblet to stare at the after cabin that held the helix. His hand made a swift gesture.

Kothar heard the guardsmen running across the deck planks in answer to that moving hand. They would be flinging open the cabin door in a moment, looking inside to see what it was that had screamed in such a bitterness of fear.

He, Kothar, also wanted a look inside the cabin.

Faster he slid downward along the golden feathers, feeling them cool to his flesh. His toes he hooked into the beak of the swan figurehead so that he dangled upside-down. His head dropped toward the cabin window.

He saw a room filled with white smoke, swirling and eddying about as if alive. Set on an ebony tripod in the fog stood a twisting spiral of thin, fine wires rising from a round blue metal base. To Kothar, it was nothing more than a toy about two feet in height. Other than the helix, the room was empty.

Where was Rufflod? Why had the thief screamed, and in such apparent agony? If the guards had not caught him—*what had?*

Kothar felt the cold sweat come out on his body. He did not hold with the forces of wizardry, and his keen nostrils smelled the stink of sorcery at the moment. The muscles in his forearms bulged as he held his grip on the cabin windowsill. All he had to do was let go his perch and vanish in the waters below, with one supple dive.

His every barbarian instinct clamored that he flee.

But a savage determination to avenge Rufflod—if he

were in fact dead—and to bring the helix with him to
the merchant Nestorius, made him grin mirthlessly. He
shifted position slowly, putting more weight on his big
hands.

It was then that the cabin door was flung open.

Upside-down, the Cumberian could see the captain
of the Prokorian Guard in gilded armor, his hard
brown face surmounted by a tall golden helmet. Peering
in past his arm was the emperor Kyros.

The emperor squealed, "Look—the window! There's
a thief hanging outside there! Somebody grab him.
Grab him!"

The guards captain ducked out of view.

Kothar gathered his muscles like the tiger before his
leap. One more moment and he would be safely away
in the cold waters. To Dwallka with the helix!

Something caught his ankles.

The barbarian let go his hold, but whatever it was
that gripped his ankles, did not. He hung upside-down
like a slab of beef in a butcher stall, trying to double up
his body to reach his feet with his hands.

Harsh laughter rang in his ears.

"Caught ourselves a crab, we have!"

"At least—some crabmeat to feed the fishes!"

"Aye—after the emperor finishes with him!"

The piping voice of Kyros could be heard from
deckside. "Bring him down, bring him down! I want to
see what manner of man dares steal from the ruler of
the world. Fetch him, I say!"

He was being raised upward on the end of a pair of
powerful ropes. An agile guard must have crept up on
the stern figurehead, dropped a noose over his feet.
Cursing, struggling, Kothar was lifted upward to the
great swan's head, scrabbling with his huge hands all
the time for a purchase on which to cling while he
kicked his feet free of the rope.

He was yanked off the swan's head. He landed with a teeth-rattling thud on the planks above the cabin. His hand shot out for a railing spoke but before he could tighten fingers on it he was jerked along, bumping and bouncing, toward the steps leading from the stern deck toward the main deck.

"A giant!"

"Yes, a barbarian from the northern lands."

"And his sword—see his sword!"

Kothar was aware that the emperor and his nobles, surrounded by guests and guardsmen, were pressing closer as he thumped and was jounced down the slanted steps to the main deck. His lips parted, baring his strong white teeth. They would not be so complacent when he kicked loose from the bindings at his ankles.

His right hand went to Frostfire in its scabbard that hung about his neck. The great blade came into the torchlight even while he was flat on his back.

A guard lunged forward, to step on it.

Twisting upward, Kothar slashed savagely, cutting into flesh and tendons as he sat up. The guard screamed, legs cut from under him.

The bloody blade sliced through ropes, freeing his ankles. Kothar came to his feet.

Everyone was crying out in terror now, except the well-trained Prokorian Guards. Fat Kyros was shrinking behind his guards captain, screeching for his men to take the giant barbarian.

Kothar yanked the belt and scabbard from around his neck, tossing the incumbrance to one side. Frostfire gleamed like blue fire in his right hand, except where its glittering length was wet with red blood.

He made a truly barbaric figure, heavily muscled, deep of chest and wide of shoulder. His long yellow hair hung down to those shoulders, and his blue eyes flared like northern ice under morning sunlight. His smile was merciless as he crouched, blade out before him.

"I want him alive," screamed Kyros.

"Forward, shields up," rasped the guards captain.

Kothar did not wait for the attack. He hurled himself sideways, toward two guards who were a little slow about raising their rectangular shields. His blade flew like a stab of lightning across the sky. Its edge bit into a soft neck, thrust sideways and darted its point into a face.

He was back where he had stood, his spine against a wall of the stern cabin, but two of the Prokorian Guards lay dead or dying at his feet.

The other guards were disciplined men, they had seen comrades die before. Their shields went up, forming a fence of metal behind which their owners half-crouched, short, stabbing swords poised in their hands.

Kothar shifted his balance. He had fought soldiers in the shield array before. He was hampered on a galley deck, he would have liked more room and firm ground under his feet, but there was enough for what he meant to do.

He ran forward. He left his feet.

His bare soles thudded into a shield. Overbalanced, the man behind it lost his footing and went down. Kothar came with him, Frostfire slashing left and then right, into the exposed backs of the guards on either side. They grunted and went down.

Kothar landed catlike on his feet.

Kyros and the guards captain were right in front of him, the emperor with his mouth open trying to scream and too terrified to make a sound. Behind him the guards were wheeling, coming for him. The big barbarian did not wait for them.

He was in front of the emperor, grabbing his flabby arm and thrusting him hard into the guards captain, stooping and getting his left arm and shoulder under the fat body of the man who ruled Avalonia. He heisted him upward easily and ran lightly toward the galley railing.

"Hold! Don't harm the emperor!" a voice roared.

"Stay your blades, stay your blades!"

Kothar gathered himself for a leap onto the railing. There, with Kyros as his hostage, he would be safe for a little while.

His feet left the deck.

In that moment of his leaping, something thudded against his head. It was not a hard blow, but it caught the big barbarian off stride. His leg buckled and he fell forward, unable to break his fall.

He saw the rail too late to avoid it.

His skull slammed hard into wood.

2

Kothar shook his head. He was on his feet, still dazed from the double blows his head had taken. His eyes opened and closed as he sought to focus his blurred vision. Gods, but Frostfire was heavy! It seemed to weigh him down as might an anchor chain.

His eyes cleared.

He was standing in front of the emperor, who sat grinning at him while his pudgy fingers fondled the great hilt of Frostfire. Kothar blinked. If Kyros held his sword, what weighted his hands so much?

He looked down at a heavy iron chain. His wrists were manacled to it, it dangled there before him, black and thick and cumbersome. While he had been unconscious, the Prokorian Guards had fettered him.

"So," Kyros said softly, "we have captured ourselves a tiger."

Kothar stared at him unwinkingly.

"What were you after, stupid man? The helix?"

Jeering laughter struck his ears. The nobles and their women crowded about, echoing the royal mirth. The barbarian stared at them, seeing the pasty faces of the men and their soft bodies hidden behind silken robes that had come by the caravan roads from beyond the Sysyphean Hills.

His eyes touched the women, flickering. Aye, these women of Avalonia were fair, their flesh smooth as

25

satin. They did not hide their bodies behind silk, they showed them proudly, half-naked in breastplates of thin gold and golden belts from which a few transparent garments floated. Their faces were regal, proud, their breasts stood up firmly, only slightly hidden by the golden cups. Excitement flared in their eyes, the desire to see a man baited, tortured and slain before them.

Kothar rumbled angrily, "I came for the helix. It will fetch me a fortune in the trade marts." He said no word of Nestorius; he felt he owed the merchant that much loyalty, since he was here to earn his gold.

Kyros barked laughter. "Fool! If you dared go into that room—but never mind that. You laid hands on my person, and for that you must die. And yet—I know not how to order your death."

"Torture him! Give him the death of the thousand cuts!"

"No—the water torture! Kyros, the water torture."

"Lash him to death at the mast!"

"Drag him below the keel as a starter."

Kyros leaned chin on fist, elbow on the arm of his throne as he studied the big barbarian. He shook his head petulantly. "No, no. None of these methods please me. I have seen men die that way. I want—something new."

Behind the emperor stood a tall, lean man, robed in black velvet covered with mystic signs and sigils. His black hair hung free to the breezes sweeping the galley deck, and there was a dark, evil look about his thin lips and narrowed eyes. Kothar knew him for a magician; probably that great necromancer Thaladomis, on whose prophecies and stargazings the emperor so depended, he whom Rufflod claimed had cheated Nestorius.

Thaladomis stirred. His dry voice rasped, "Slay him out of hand, sire—or he will be your doom! I vow this, on the silent voices of the stars which speak to me."

"I heed your counsel in all things, Thaladomis. But not in this. No! My party was lagging, that dancer from Oasia ruined it with her stupid posturings. Where did she run to, the slut? Eh? Fetch her, someone!"

Thaladomis shook his head glumly, but he made no other protest except to make a sorcerous sign in the air. Gazing steadily at him, Kothar saw the air turn faintly red about that moving finger.

Bare feet padded on the deck planks and the Oasian dancing girl was flung forward by a Prokorian Guard. She was very lovely, Kothar thought, staring down into her dusky face and the thick black hair that framed it. Her red mouth, full and open in her fear, was enriched by henna. Her slanted eyes touched the big barbarian, then she went to her knees before the emperor.

"Great lord, I did my best," she whispered.

"Your best is not good enough for Kyros. For the ruler of the world, you must do better than that!"

Kyros was leaning forward, eyes bright. "What? Still in that cloak that covers you from toes to head? You wore enough clothing while you danced, but to see you shrouded like a mummy out of Aegypton turns my blood cold. Are you too lovely for my eyes and the eyes of my noble men and women to see?"

"No, lord," she whimpered, head bent low.

"Then off with the cloak. Off with it, I say!"

Her trembling fingers loosed the strings. A hand reached out from the crowd and caught it, yanking it off her body. She knelt there in her dancing costume, fine legs bare to hips, a mere length of silk tied about her loins and dangling between her thighs.

Kothar blinked. The girl was all but naked.

Kyros gestured impatiently. "The rest of it, the rest of it! Am I served by dead men? Strip her down, the clumsy slut!"

A hand caught her thick black hair, tugged her to

her feet. Other hands seized the tinted dancing silks that were her only garment. In a moment she shrank naked against Kothar, as if imploring him for help.

"Look at them—beauty and her beast!" Kyros jeered.

He paused suddenly and lifted a great, flat emerald to his eye. Through it he squinted at the couple, his thick lips curving into a smile.

"I have it, I have it! We shall sentence the both of them together. Hey? Is not your ruler a genius? A twin death for twin annoyances!"

Excited voices babbled praise for Kyros, ruler of the world. The emperor sank back against the high back of the ivory throne, a pleased smile on his petulant mouth, nodding to himself. Two soldiers stepped forward in answer to his gesture.

"Seize the wench, strap her to his back," he ordered.

The numbed dancing girl was lifted high, swung down so her body fell atop the broad back of the Cumberian. Kothar quivered at that touch of female flesh, but he made no other move, standing as might a giant rock while straps were brought and her wrists and arms fastened to his own thick wrists and heavily muscled biceps.

A broader strap was brought and her middle was tied against his own, just above the loincloth he wore. Smaller thongs were used to fasten her shapely legs to his thickly thewed thighs and calves.

They stood there, when the Prokorian Guards were done, like some strange and monstrous beast. The men and women crowding about were interested, all of them eager to see the sharp edge of the imperial whimsy. They waited almost breathlessly.

"You can protect your back, barbarian—by letting Laella take the punishment while you try to save both your skins. However, if she is harmed, the fight shall be stopped and you shall be strung up and whipped.

"Now—bring out Gorth!"

A roar went up from the courtiers and their women crowding about the throne. To one side, there was a creak of rolling wheels, a deep rumble, and then a cage with silver bars came into view.

A sob sounded in Kothar's ear. "Gorth! He will kill us both together! He will fasten his claws in my back and—"

Kothar tried to stare between the pressing bodies of the men and women. What manner of beast was this Gorth? There was no sound, no snarl nor coughing rumble that might tell him whether the thing inside the bars was leopard or lion.

Two women drew apart, suddenly.

Through the space where they had stood, the barbarian could see the oncoming cage and the huge, hairy body inside it. A bear! A great brown bear from the mountains known as the Roof of The World. These brown bears were gigantic beasts, and although Kothar had never seen one, he knew they towered eight feet from claw to furry ears when standing on their hind legs.

His skin crawled. Alone and unburdened, he would have had a hard time staying alive against such an opponent. Tethered by chains in front and by a naked woman on his back, his task was all but hopeless. Yet a savage rumble began deep in his throat as his eyes met the small eyes of the giant bear, standing erect behind the silver bars now, sensing its momentary freedom.

The bear made a small, angry thunder in its hairy chest as it studied the big man it was to slay. Other times, other faces, Gorth had known, when his master had brought him out to fight picked slaves for the amusement of the men and women his master entertained. Gorth shifted uneasily on its paws, he had never fought on a ship before, and though the waters of Lake Lotusine were calm and placid, the galley did roll slightly, and this troubled the big bear.

A grate of metal, and the barred door rose. Gorth lumbered out onto the deck planks, its huge head turning this way and then that, as its nostrils grew to know these man-smells and female perfumes. Then its head lowered and its ears pricked forward. It eyed the strange thing it was to kill.

Gorth rose upward, eight feet and a few inches of furred savagery, studying the man and woman fastened together, rumbling angrily in its throat. They did not look so dangerous. True, the man was crouching, putting his hands together to gather the heavy iron chains in his hands so it made a dangling length of black metal, but otherwise he did not seem so formidable. At least, he did not hold one of those shining lengths of sharp metal whose bite Gorth had tasted in the past, during a fight.

The bear dropped to all fours, shuffled forward.

Kothar waited quietly, tensed and motionless on bent legs. He must not let the animal put its arms about him. It might well crush both Laella and him to death, if it were allowed to—

"Hai!" he bellowed, leaping.

The black chain whipped like a leather thong in his great hands. Its links drove down and onto the furred head. There was a crunch, a ripping sound, and when the chain was yanked away, a strip of fur and red blood went with it.

Gorth reared up, roaring with pain and fury.

"First blood to the barbarian!" screamed a woman.

Kyros was leaning forward on his throne, eyes brilliant. His spirit thrilled to such unequal contests, because his was not the soul of the sportsman who reveled in a battle between well-matched opponents, but that of a weakling who delights in seeing another human being, more powerful and braver than he, go down before too-great-odds.

Kothar bounded catlike away from a return swipe with a huge paw that Gorth sent out at him. He circled on bare feet, making the animal turn. The chain was ready in his hands, it was a great weight but it was not too much for his muscles. For a little while, at least.

He knew he would tire in time. With Laella on his back and the chains about his wrists, he could not long continue this fight.

There might be a chance, however.

If he could madden the beast, divert it from its primary target, it might go berserk and attack anyone within claw-reach. Kothar tensed, leaped again.

His foot hit a little pool of blood, landing on the torn bit of fur the chain had ripped from Gorth's head. Kothar lost his balance, fell heavily on his side.

Laella screamed, taking part of that fall.

Gorth dropped toward his victims, long claws extended.

Kothar rolled over, under the extended forelegs. His hands shot up, gripped the fur on the side of the bear, yanked upward. Gorth swiped at him, but missed, and then Kothar was rising, planting himself on his bare feet.

The bear lifted into the air, towering above the manthing.

Fast was Kothar, like lightning his movements. He had fought the great white bears of the northern ice wastes in his youth, with spear and club, he knew the speed of the beasts and their weaknesses.

In this moment of its rising, the bear could not protect its face. The heavy chain whipped sideways, through the air like a flail, cutting down across the little red eyes.

Gorth screamed in agony as those links bit deep.

Kothar was in and out, gathering up the chain, waiting as he panted for the beast to come for him again. The bear was in too much agony for this, it rubbed at its bleeding eyes with its paws, it made small, whimpering sounds from its froth-flecked jaws.

In a moment, Gorth would feel the pain, when the shock wore off. Then indeed, would he go mad. Slowly, step by step, the barbarian backed away from the beast. On top of him, Laella moaned. Her long black hair hung over his shoulders, tickling his sweating flesh when the wind blew. Her body shook steadily.

She stirred, moving her head. The Cumberian could hear her indrawn breath rasp in sudden terror.

"What happened?" she asked.

"I've blinded him—I think."

"Even if you kill it, what good will it do?"

Kothar showed his teeth in a cold grin. "Can you swim, girl?"

"Like a fish, usually. But this way—fastened to you— I am not sure. You cannot carry me—and the chain, in the water."

"Hssssst!"

Gorth was making roaring sounds now, lifting a bloody face and opening its jaws. The bear could see, faintly, as through a bloody film, but it felt far more the stabs of pain driving like red-hot pokers into its skull, taking away its reason.

Forgotten were its opponents, all it wanted at this moment was to pay back humankind for this agony it had given him. It sniffed the air about him. Humankind was everywhere, soft and weak and perfumed.

Gorth lunged. Great jaws opened and closed on a man in the bright silks of a nobleman of the court of

Kyros. Flesh and bone cracked as he bit deep. At the same time, a right forearm shot out, claws bedding themselves in female flesh and ripping.

Kyros was on his feet, quivering in terror.

"Slay it, slay the beast!"

A dozen Prokorian Guards leaped to obey, spears out and stabbing, shields up to protect themselves from the clawed fury that ravened on the deck planks. Everywhere, men and women were turning to run, witless in their terror.

Nobody remembered Kothar.

The barbarian had backed up until Laella's spine was rammed into the cold metal of a guardsman's shield. He felt her stiffen from that contact, then he was whirling, setting both hands to that shield and the shield to its left, yanking them apart.

Kothar was between and past the startled guardsmen, running on bare feet for the rail. He knew he risked a thrown javelin that might impale both the girl and himself, but if he did not make this attempt, certain death remained for him on the galley deck.

He did not bother to put foot on the rail molding.

He dove over the balustrade, flattened out.

A spear went past his shoulder. Then he was falling for the blackish waters, arms out in front of him. Atop him, he felt the softness of Laella's naked body tighten as she steeled her flesh to the shock of entry into that water.

They hit the water and went down into Stygian blackness. Deep they went, dragged along by the heavy chain, but Kothar and Laella were used to swimming, each had taken a deep breath before splashing down. They began to swim in unison, as if their minds were locked together; actually, the dancing girl took her cues from the powerfully muscled body of the blond barbarian, as if she danced with him.

They moved upward, slowly, slowly, for the weight
of the chain was awful, and their human lungs could
scarcely contain enough air to counterbalance its drag.
Yet they succeeded, their wet hands bobbing into view
a few yards from the galley.

They could hear the screams of the women, the
shouts of the men aboard the galley, and the more
thunderous roars of Gorth, biting, striking, slaying as
he moved through a red haze of pain against these
man-things, one of whom had hurt him.

To Laella's amazement, Kothar struck out for the
galley.

"Are you mad?" she asked, moving arms and legs
with his.

His hands went up, stabbed at an oarblade. Hand
over hand, he moved along the oars, knowing full well
that the slaves chained to these oars were deep in sleep,
snatching what slumber they could while their owners
were busy overhead with their entertainments.

"We have to cut free of each other," Kothar growled.

He reached the last oar, sought for a handgrip on the
carvings decorating the apostis, that part of the galley
jutting outward above the bulwarks. He swung on these
carvings, his body straining to the utmost with the
weight of chain and girl, until he touched the lower
part of the ram, which thrust forward a foot above the
water.

"Hang on, now," he panted.

The girl did her best to fasten fingers on the carvings. Her breath sobbed in her throat, her long hair
floated in the cold waters. She managed to get
handgrips, and she sought to hang there, freeing
Kothar's hands. He had tossed the heavy chain over the
ram, so it did not drag on them too much.

He was working his long, strong fingers on the strap
fittings. The straps were buckled, she saw, and after a

moment of fierce tugging, the buckle parted. She sagged downward, her strength hardly enough to keep her body afloat. Luckily, her middle and her legs were still tied to those of this giant barbarian.

Her other arm was free; she felt his feet fumbling for toeholds on the rough boarding of the beak; to ease her weight on his back, she threw the arm over the ram. When he got his feet securely wedged into niches, it made it easier for him to undo the buckle on his left wrist.

"I belong to you," Laella whispered, kissing his shoulder.

Kothar grunted. "You belong to yourself, girl."

"You freed me from my master. They would ha-have tor-tortured me up there, if the bear hadn't killed me. Kyros does that at times, claiming that certain slaves of merchants do not please him and demanding they be punished by some sort of awful death, to amuse himself and his court.

"Of course, afterward, he makes a recompense of sorts to the merchants, for he enjoys his little entertainments and he knows if he is too severe, no traders will bring any more trained animals or dancing girls to Romm."

Kothar felt her breasts move as her shoulders shrugged. "That does the dead slave no good, but it insures that Kyros will have plenty of pretty slavegirls to make die in convulsions of agony before his gloating eyes.

"I hate Kyros!"

Kothar grinned, "Good. I despise him, myself. That is why I am going to take his precious helix away from him."

He felt her body stiffen against his as he unbuckled the strap about their middles. "Take the helix? You must be mad! Do you know what that is, that helix? I heard the mage Thaladomis speak of it, to my master."

She shivered. He waited, then muttered, "Well? What is it?"

His fingers worked on the straps holding their legs together as she breathed, "It is a magical doorway into—into some other world. It gives off a white radiance. Wrapped in a cloak, Kyros can enter that radiance, which destroys human flesh and bones, otherwise. He disappears, still wearing the cloak, and wanders amid lands of strange and terrible beauty. Inside the cloak, he is safe from danger in that other world, which Thaladomis calls Nirvalla."

The last strap fell away.

Kothar put his arm about the shivering girl and hoisted her up to the ram, plopping her down so she sat there, both hands fastened to the bronze plates covering that long wooden beak. Her eyes were enormous, staring down at him.

"You don't mean it? You're not really going after the helix?"

"You're safe, you can swim to shore from here."

"I can't leave you. I belong to you."

Kothar grinned and clapped her wet thigh with a big hand. "Then wait for me, girl. I won't be long. If Kyros has a cloak, I mean to take it away from him just as I'll take away the helix."

Like a big cat he began to climb the curving prow of the golden galley, hand over hand and with his toes seeking holds by stabbing blindly. Upward he went with pantherish ease as the naked girl clung to the ram and watched.

His head lifted above the cabin window. Not daring to enter the cabin where Rufflod had disappeared so mysteriously, he waited, patient as a tiger on the prowl. He heard the sound of voices, the sharp cries and grunts of fighting men, the bellowing of a wounded, blinded bear as it sought to take as many human lives as it could before the stabbing swords of the guardsmen reached its heart.

Now he could hear the emperor, babbling with fright.

"Around me! Form a ring around me, get me to the stern cabin," Kyros cried.

A man screamed as the bear clawed his face. Then the measured tramp of disciplined guards told Kothar the emperor was being herded toward the cabin door. The Cumberian shifted his weight on his bare feet. His hands raised the long chain to which he was still manacled.

The cabin door opened.

Kyros stood framed for a moment against the torchlight visible through that long rectangular doorway. A thick scarlet cloak, marked with mystic symbols worked in silver thread, had been tossed about his shoulders. A cowl, decorated by runes and amulets pinned to its surface, shadowed the emperor's face until only a white blob was visible.

Kyros moved into the room of the white mists. From the window, Kothar watched with wide eyes, half-expecting him to vanish as Rufflod had vanished. The emperor walked straight forward toward the helix, cloak wrapped tightly about him.

Balanced on his toes, his hands and arms free, Kothar waited.

The chain of black links was gathered in his two hands. Kyros was close, now. A long sweep of that chain would hit him, stun him.

Another few steps, and Kyros would be in range.

The barbarian rose up, hurled his chain. Below him the water rippled at the stern. A false move would overbalance him, send him down into those cold waters. But Kothar had a body trained to cling to small perches since boyhood, when he had hunted mountain goats in Cumberia. His leg muscles swelled. He hung there, casting that chain into the room of the white fogs.

The links hit the cowl.

The cowl crumpled, caught in the black links. It leaped as Kothar made the chain leap backward toward him. The cloak with the magic sigils seemed almost to fly through the air at him.

Where Kyros had been—was nothingness!

Only the white mist floated there. The emperor of Avalonia was gone. Kothar gulped, catching the cloak and dragging it through the window.

Hurriedly, he threw the cloak about him, feeling its material send a tingling shock through his flesh. Grunting against this seeming result of magical incantations, he drew the cowl down about his head, wondering if Kyros still had the sword Frostfire, if he had suffered Rufflod's fate, or if he wandered somewhere in that hidden world Laella had named Nirvalla.

He threw a leg, protected by the cloak, over the sill. He stepped into the room. Kothar saw, as he wrapped himself deeper in the folds of the cloak, that the mists seemed thinner. The helix still blazed with a golden refulgence, looked at from the shadowed recesses of the cowl, but the white fog was dissipating.

He strode forward.

Hands outstretched, he reached for the helix.

There was a blaze of white-hot brilliance, and Kothar felt the floor go out from under his bare feet. He poised a moment in that yellow radiance, floating between the opening corners of reality.

And then—

A face appeared before him.

"Red Lori!" he bellowed.

Mocking laughter shook him, inside the protective

cloak. Her eyes were wide, gleeful, taunting. He noticed her long red lashes, like tiny fans, that seemed to regard him as if he were some kind of pet.

"Yes, Kothar, my hated one, my foe! I am Red Lori. Oh, don't worry—I'm safely locked behind silver bars, I still hang from the ceiling in Queen Elfa's audience hall. But my spirit can go where I will it—and I will it now to let you see it.

"Foolish man! Did you think the words I spoke were empty as the breeze that sweeps across the meadows? I meant them, Kothar!

"When you overcame me and put me here, you earned my hate. You belong to me, barbarian—to be punished. I have not chosen yet to punish you—but be punished you will, in time. So for now, go into Nirvalla—but know that I go with you in spirit. What happens to you will be the result of what I want to happen!"

Her laughter rang out again, from the red mouth that formed a wide oval, so that Kothar could see her tongue. Her slanted green eyes blazed with mockery.

Then she was gone.

Kothar felt something firm into existence under his feet.

3

He stood on a flat rock, above a rolling grassland that stretched away toward low hills and a forested slope in the distance. Closer, where he stood with the cloak flapping in the warm wind, rocks were piled high as though a giant hand had flung them together in a playful mood.

The sky was yellow here, and the wind seemed to whisper as with many soft voices. Almost, it seemed he could understand those voices. They warned him, they counseled him, but he could not understand their words, only the mood they wrote across his mind with their faint suspirations. A shadow moved along the ground. Looking up, he saw a giant eagle soaring along on the wind currents, with widespread wings.

Kothar shook himself.

There was a black tower in the distance, and a narrow roadway leading to it, past the rock pile where the barbarian stood. He moved down, walked along to the road. There would be someone in the tower, he hoped, who could tell him where he was and how to get back into the room with the helix.

It seemed he had walked for only a little while, then the tower loomed before him, squat and low, with the mark of ineffable age on its dark stones. There were no windows in the tower, none that he could see, at least.

Only a great oaken door, hung with an iron knocker, showed that there was any way in or out of that tower.

Kothar gripped the knocker, banged it hard.

The door opened soundlessly. A woman in a tight black kirtle stood there, her face white as chalk, her lips the color of fresh red blood, her eyes behind long black lashes and thin brows like burning black coals. She did not seemed surprised to see him, her lips curled into a faint smile.

"Whom seek you, stranger?"

"The emperor of Avalonia, Kyros. He has my sword Frostfire. I would win it back from him."

The woman stood back, nodding. "Enter, then. I am Leithe, of this land Nirvalla. I know of Kyros and his golden galley where he keeps the helix."

Kothar moved into the hall, his bare feet touching the curious stones that formed the tower floor. Though they appeared cold, the flaggings, each one marked with a magical sign, were quite warm and comfortable. The walls were draped in thick brocades of scarlet and black, with the signs of the Seven Sisters of Salathus worked into their materials. An iron torchere on the wall held a length of glowing wood that gave off a surprising amount of bluish light.

The woman walked ahead of him, her rounded haunches swaying with catlike grace as she led the way into a room beyond the hall. Here was set a long banqueting table, with crystal goblets and platters of earthenware.

"Eat, stranger. While you dine, I will tell you a little tale," Leithe murmured, moving to the table, lifting the cover from a platter and revealing steaming meat, gesturing at a salver piled with bread, removing the top of a plate that held several cheeses.

She poured red wine into a crystal goblet for him as Kothar seated himself on a bench. Her black eyes studied his great body, nodding from time to time as she mentally assayed the strength in his rolling muscles.

"You may be the one," she told him as he reached for meat and bread. "Long have I waited for you to come walking down that road."

"The one for what?" the Cumberian asked, between bites.

"The man to break the spell of Thaladomis."

Kothar blinked, head lifting with surprise. "The emperor's magician? What's he got to do with Nirvalla?"

The woman seated herself at the table, reached for a crystal goblet and sipped at the red wine it contained. Her eyes brooded as she looked back into the past.

"This world of Nirvalla was created by the arch-mage Phronalom.

"Phronalom was the greatest wizard of his time. Only the almost mythical Afgorkon was his better, it is said. Phronalom lived in the kingdom of Althasia, long and long ago, perhaps forty thousand of your years."

The barbarian nodded, wiping his wine-wet lips with the back of his hairy forearm. "I've heard of Althasia and of Phronalom. They tell fairy tales about them in Vandacia."

The woman began to talk.

Althasia in those days was a world of tyrants and warlords, of armies marching to conquest, of soldiers in little bands breaking into the homes of citizens, carrying them off with their wives and children to serve the desires of King Drongol. To King Drongol, his people existed only to pleasure his royal whims and fulfill the needs of his kingdom.

He established breeding farms where his most valiant warriors acted as studs to the healthiest and loveliest women of the kingdom. Children and more children, demanded the king. Male children, to train as warriors, female children to bear more future warriors.

Phronalom lived in Althasia, content with his magic and his beloved wife, Ayatha. Ayatha was reputedly the most beautiful woman in the world at that time. On her, King Drongol cast a wanting eye. Not for himself, he had concubines by the hundreds to assuage his lusts; he wanted Ayatha for his breeding farms, for she was as wise as she was beautiful.

By his spells, Phronalom learned of this plan, and decided to thwart it. None could match him for his esoteric knowledge, his understanding of necromancies and the dark wisdoms. Though King Drongol had surrounded himself with wizards, Phronalom was the greatest of them all.

On a wild night, when lightning shredded the sky with yellow flashes and the rains poured down like the tears of the gods, Phronalom summoned up the demon spirits who served him. On these incubi, he asked a simple question. How could he escape the evil schemes of Drongol?

The demons told him he must build a helix.

The helix would be the doorway into a world that the helix itself, by means of the necromantic spells and cantraips by which it was formed, would create. Into that world—Nirvalla—Phronalom and Ayatha could flee, and with them such retainers and acquaintances as might choose to make the journey.

In his sorcerous sanctuary, Phronalom performed the rites to make the helix. It took seven hours, even with the demons of Ebthor and Nixus to help him. During these seven hours, the soldiers of King Drongol came for Ayatha. To the pounding of their spear-butts on the door, Phronalom finished his incantation.

The golden helix glowed for the first time.

Into Nirvalla, this land of magical enchantment, stepped Phronalom and his wife, with many of their servitors and their acquaintances. It was a lush, young world, as Yarth itself might have been before the coming of man. The winds were sweet, the grasses rich and lush, the trees heavily leaved so that when the wind stirred them their branches made music like that of a thousand harps. The water of this magical world was sweet, the meats of its animals tasty.

Here lived the great mage, happily untouched by human hates and greeds and lusts. The land he gave freely to his friends. There was so much of it, no man or woman would be crowded, and with his cantrips, Phronalom could always extend its borders.

"There is no age in Nirvalla, no Time," smiled Leithe, refilling their crystal cups. "For close to forty thousand of your years we have dwelt here, in a kind of paradise.

"We can conjure up what we want, out of the very air, for Nirvalla is a land of sorcery, and that very sorcery seems to be alive in the air."

Kothar swallowed his wine and pushed away his empty platter. His hand went automatically to where Frostfire usually hung in its scabbard, but when his fingers closed on empty air, he frowned.

"What of Kyros? How did he get the helix?" he asked.

Leithe smiled sadly.

"Thaladomis is a mighty mage. He was born in Vandacis, in that land which was known once as Althasia. He had heard of the great Phronalom, and devoted his early years to tracking down old parchments and palimpsests which told of his enchantments. In dusty cellars and forgotten tombs he came upon these relics of a forgotten age."

Studying the scrolls, Thaladomis realized that he could himself venture into Nirvalla, perhaps even steal the helix. However, he was magician enough to know that the helix would be guarded by terrible spells, and first he must find a way to counteract those sorceries.

Long he hunted, until at last, beside the white dust of what had been a skeleton centuries ago, he came upon a length of parchment which, protected by necromancies, had endured through the years. The parchment told how each member of the little group who had gone into Nirvalla with Phronalom and Ayatha wore magic cloaks that protected them from the baneful influence of the helix.

Creating such a cloak for himself with the aid of certain demons who hated the demons of Ebthor and Nixus, Thaladomis went himself into Nirvalla. He found the helix, and spoke the word that would enable him to touch it.

With the helix, Thaladomis went from Nirvalla into his own world. The prize was his, but when he had finished gloating over it, Thaladomis realized he was no better off than he was before. He could go in or out of Nirvalla, but what good would that do him? He was a man who enjoyed life, the kisses of women and their caresses, the taste of rare foods and fine wines, and the helix would give him none of these.

Still, there must be a man in his world who would pay him well for the helix, for the privilege of going into Nirvalla and enjoying its eternal youthfulness. For two years, Thaladomis pondered, then he decided on a prospective buyer, at the suggestion of a merchant named Nestorius.

Avalonia was the richest kingdom in all Yarth.

The emperor Kyros was its richest man.

To Kyros then, went Thaladomis, with the helix. He permitted Kyros to don the cloak and walk into the hidden lands, and when he emerged, Kyros was exultant. He offered Thaladomis a fortune in gold and jewels, he built Thaladomis a palace only slightly less luxurious than his own. The magician was given his pick of the beautiful women of his court.

Leithe laughed harshly. "That fat man, coming here and going when and where he would, in perfect safety! Phronalom does not dare harm him, for fear Thaladomis might destroy the helix in retaliation.

"And if that happens—"

"Nirvalla is no more!"

Leithe stared down into her empty goblet, turning it around and around with her slender fingers. "You might think forty thousand years is a long time, stranger. It is no more than the winking of an eyelid to us who enjoy the pleasures of Nirvalla."

Her black eyes rose to study his big, muscular body. "We have all we want here, except age and misery. If I want a youth for my enjoyment, all I need to do is—"

Her slim white fingers made certain signs in the air.

A young man in a short chiton stood before them, golden locks on his head, a small harp in his hands. Leithe stared at him with warm eyes.

"Vathik," she smiled. "He loves me. And he plays the harp beautifully, almost as well as fabled Otheron."

Her fingers wriggled, the youth disappeared. Leithe sighed. Kothar grinned at her bent head. "I can see why you enjoy this kind of life—but it isn't for me. I'd rust from idleness. Give me Frostfire and a way back to my own world and time, and I'll be grateful."

Leithe lifted her head, staring at him.

"You could be the one," she said at last. "You see, when Thaladomis stole the helix, he was forced by the very nature of the demoniac magic that went into the creation of the helix to cast a spell in its place.

"By his spell, Thaladomis placed Ayatha herself in thrall for the helix. If the helix is returned to Nirvalla— Ayatha dies!"

Kothar growled, "Then how in the name of great Dwallka can I help? How can anyone help?"

A scarlet fingernail traced a little sign on the bare wooden tabletop. "There is a way," murmured Leithe. "It needs a brave man, a man with a crazy, mad kind of courage. But it can be done."

"The spell involves the demon Warrl. By trickery, Thaladomis imprisoned Warrl inside a great ruby on which the necromancies that control the return of the helix to Nirvalla as well as the life or death of Ayatha are engraved. Shatter that ruby—and you release the demon inside it and render useless the incantations that prevent the return of the helix. Shattered, the ruby spell that decides whether Ayatha lives or dies is also rendered null and void. The trouble is—no one knows where the ruby is hidden but Thaladomis himself."

Kothar nodded, "That's easy to understand—but first I must find Kyros."

The woman frowned. "Why Kyros? He is nothing!"

"He carries Frostfire," Kothar grinned coldly, showing his big white teeth. "And I mean to have my sword back."

Leithe laughed softly. "I can show you a dozen swords, give them all to you—come with me!"

She rose with a supple twisting of her slim body beneath the clinging black stuff of her gown. A beautiful woman was Leithe the enchantress and at another time, Kothar told himself, he might be interested in teaching her how a man who did not disappear at the flick of the fingers might please her fleshly needs far better than Vathik.

Following her twitching buttocks out into the hall and up a flight of wooden steps, Kothar came to the round tower room where Leithe performed her own incantations. There were vials and parchments here; in the cabinets about the walls were the dried wings of bats, the hairs of cats, the many artifacts needed for her spells. On several prie-dieux were open volumes containing the lore of a thousand wizards.

On a golden tripod, set into a velvet-lined ring, was a large silver ball. The surface of the globe was highly polished, so that it hurt the eyes to gaze upon it. Leithe crossed to the ball, touched it with her fingers. Kothar saw that high gloss vanish so that the ball became transparent as crystal. In it, little black wisps of smoke appeared to float.

"Gaze, stranger!" Leithe whispered.

There was a tiny sword inside the globe, a great, two-handed weapon with a glittering blade that glistened as if sunlight touched it. "Jortos swung that blade, Jortos the hero of Alvia, in his defence of his homeland. It is yours, if you say the word."

Her fingers moved again and the two-handed sword was replaced by a curved scimitar with a red velvet-wrapped hilt in which gleamed a blue jewel. "Salamor used that sword when he destroyed the demon gods of Oasia. If you want it, nod your head."

"Frostfire was made by Afgorkon," the barbarian rumbled. "Afgorkon gave it to me to help Queen Elfa. I feel naked without it. I want only Frostfire."

"And Kyros carries that sword?" Leithe asked.

Her palm went down on the globe, pressed it. Her blued eyelids closed so that her lashes made little black fans on her cheeks. She seemed almost not to breathe, to be no more than a wax mannikin of a woman for a few seconds.

"Look," she breathed.

Inside the globe, Kyros sat on a flat rock that bordered a limpid pool in which naiads swam, laughing and sporting with one another. Two of them, naked, were holding bunches of purple grapes to Kyros' lips, bidding him swallow this fruit of Nirvalla.

Leithe whispered, "The grapes give him youthfulness to carry into his world. He has been here before, that man. He is almost as deadly as Thaladomis, for he intends to bring soldiers here—and to make Nirvalla his own where he will rule forever.

"He is a wicked, evil man. He would destroy our peace." Leithe sighed, nodding. "Yes, perhaps it is best that you go to Kyros and take Frostfire away from him." She held up a warning finger. "But I must tell you one thing. You cannot kill Kyros in Nirvalla. He is protected by the same spell that keeps us all young. There is no death here, and the man who tries to kill another—dies himself."

Kothar growled, "By Dwallka! You try a man's patience with all these limitations on what a man may do. Very well! I'll heed you—but can I choke him, just a little?"

The woman laughed, throwing back her head.

"Yes, Kothar—choke him, but not unto death!"

Her right hand lifted. It made signs at the giant barbarian. Kothar felt cold, as if he were embedded inside the great glacier that lay astride parts of Cumberia and Thuum in his northland home. In that cold, his chains turned to powder, blew away.

He gasped for breath—

Kyros was five feet away, nibbling at the grapes the naked naiads fed him. In its jeweled scabbard, Frostfire lay propped between his knees. Kothar tensed on the rock where he stood, about to make his leap.

The emperor looked slimmer, stronger, to his eyes, and he realized that the grapes were feeding his flesh with youth and strength. He was not so much the fat fop now as he was a younger, more vital man. The jewels he wore on his fingers, the great emerald hanging in its golden circlet from his throat, seemed almost out of place.

Kothar began his leap.

Kyros saw him from the corners of his eyes. He sprang aside, thrusting a naiad between himself and the barbarian. At the same time his right hand moved down to grip Frostfire's hilt and yank free the blued blade.

The naiad screamed as her falling body hit Kothar just below the knees, toppling him forward. The barbarian fell heavily, almost at the feet of the youthful emperor.

Up came that great blade, poised to strike.

Kothar cried, "Wait! There is a curse on that steel, Kyros!"

The wind had been knocked from his great body so that the Cumberian could only lie there and drag in mouthsful of air into his lungs as Kyros lowered the point of the blade and touched it to his throat.

"What curse, barbarian? Tell me before I slay you—and tell me also how you came into this hidden land! I paid Thaladomis well for that privilege! If every thief in Avalonia can cross over into Nirvalla, I'll begin to think the mage cheated me!"

Kothar grunted against the point digging into his neckflesh. "I hooked the cloak with my chain, just as you disappeared. But that's of no importance. What is important is the fact that no man who owns Frostfire can own any other wealth!"

The emperor laughed, quite good-naturedly. "Liar! See my jewels. Study the emerald eyeglass I carry about my neck. Men would die to own those things, they are worth small kingdoms, of themselves."

"They are glass," grinned Kothar.

Kyros, slightly startled, glanced at his left hand where he wore three rings. At the same time he pressed the point deeper into Kothar's throat, so that it drew a speck of blood from his sun-bronzed flesh.

"Liar! They are—"

Frantically, Kyros held his left hand higher so the yellow light of Nirvalla struck it, showed the jewels in his rings to be lusterless and dull. Flushing with disbelief, the emperor clawed at the great emerald in its golden filigreework at the end of his neck-chain.

And Kothar struck.

His arm hit the blade, knocked it sideways.

He came rolling off a hip, driving his massively muscled body into the emperor's legs. Back went Kyros, to thud down hard on the grassy bank. Before the man could move, Kothar leaped. His powerful fingers went deep into his fat throat as he flung himself astraddle across his body. Those mighty fingers tightened.

Kyros tried to scream, but could not.

His eyes bulged, his fat cheeks shook, his mouth was a huge, distorted circle of bluish lips. The flabby hands that had been caressing the naked naiads were now writhing at the iron-hard wrists bearing the weight of those suffocating hands deeper, deeper into his throat.

Then Kothar grinned, and let his fingers relax a little. Kyros made a whistling sound in his throat as he dragged air into his lungs.

The barbarian growled, "Do you want to die?"

Frantically, Kyros shook his head. "No," he whimpered. "No, no—have mercy, Kothar!"

"I will have mercy, Kyros—if you tell me of the spell Thaladomis wove to enable him to keep the helix out of Nirvalla."

It was a long shot he was betting on, the Cumberian knew, but he understood men, and as sly a ruler as Kyros would never have committed his precious person into the safekeeping of as strange a world as Nirvalla without some assurance that he was safe. Kyros would have demanded, when he paid the price for the helix, reassurances that he would be unharmed in this magic land.

Thaladomis would have told him of the ensorcelled ruby and of the spell the mage had put upon it which would make the helix safe from removal back into Nirvalla. The necromancer would have boasted of his slyness in hiding that jewel so its spell could not be removed but the emperor would have wheedled the information out of him. The flicker of understanding in Kyros' eyes told him he was right.

Kyros panted, "I—I don't know."

Iron fingers tightened once again. Kyros beat the air with his plump, perfumed hands, making movements with his blue lips. "Wa-wait," he gasped. "Perhaps I do remember."

Kothar took away his hand. Kyros lay there gasping, moving his head from right to left and back again. There were big purple blotches on his neck.

"Thaladomis locked a powerful demon inside the ruby gem of Gwanthol," Kyros babbled. "The jewel he hid in the—in the belly of Skrye, the great eagle of Nirvalla."

"An eagle?" Kothar rumbled.

Kyros nodded, smiling a wicked grin. "Yes, an eagle created by a spell of the magician, an eagle nothing can harm. Skrye flies high, barbarian—in the cold reaches of the clouds, where no man and no arrow can go."

As if in mockery, an eagle screamed, high up where the sky made a blue vault, specked with distant clouds. Kothar knelt astride the emperor of Avalonia, and knew disgust. He could never hope to catch and slay that eagle. His keen eyes picked out the tiny white dot soaring there, and he sighed.

His quest was hopeless.

4

Leithe laughed when he told her what Kyros had said. They sat once again in her dining hall, Kothar eating meat and quaffing great gulps of the chilled red wine at which Leithe merely sipped. Her black eyes were alight with triumph.

"There is a way, now that we know where the ruby is hidden," she comforted him. "All we need do is make a plan to catch it."

"And then, what?" the barbarian growled. "Nothing dies, here in Nirvalla! You told me so, yourself. How do I get the ruby out of Skrye except by disemboweling him—and if the bird is to live on in agony—well, I don't know."

Leithe laughed again. "Only those who crossed over with Phronalom are protected by his magic. Skrye was created by Thaladomis, and no such protection clings to him. No, no. You may slay Skrye—if you can."

The woman frowned, suddenly thoughtful. She repeated softly, "If you can. Yes! For Thaladomis must have placed a powerful spell on Skrye, to save it from some such venture as you would attempt."

"If I could not slay Kyros for fear of dying myself, why can I kill Skrye?" Kothar wondered.

"Kyros is a man, Skyre is but an animal. There are different rules for each." Leithe smiled faintly. "If we could not kill animals here in Nirvalla, what would we do for our meals? No, no, if you can slay Skrye, you may, safely."

She brooded, forgetful of the man, until at last she sighed and shook her head so that her long ebon tresses danced. "I do not know the way," she confessed.

Kothar chuckled, putting a hand on the jeweled hilt of Frostfire, drawing it upward in its scabbard until the woman could see its polished blue blade. "My Frostfire will find a way. Afgorkon made it, there is magic in that steel—a rare and terrible magic."

He swallowed more wine, pouring it this time himself, from the big silver pitcher. He muttered, with his goblet halfway to his lips, "All I need to do is find Skrye, to get him down to the ground. Dwallka knows I can't go flying through the air the way he does."

Leithe nodded, "In that, at least, I can help. When Thaladomis left Skrye in Nirvalla, it was as a real eagle, with the wants of an eagle. With something like our present needs in mind, we of Nirvalla have been feeding young lambs to Skrye, so that by now he comes unsuspectingly to a farmstead some miles from here, to feed when the hunger moves in him.

"He does not always feed at the farm, but he does come more or less regularly, seeming to know that tender food will be there for the mere taking. You shall go there, Kothar—and wait for Skrye."

The barbarian yawned. "I'm tired," he confessed.

Leithe rose to her feet. "You shall sleep in my bed, stranger. I have me a mind to test the muscles of your body, and its strength."

Kothar grinned, wiping his wine-wet lips with the back of a huge forearm where golden hairs glittered in the torchlight. "I'm tired, Leithe. When I sleep, I sleep. But I do thank you for the offer."

Leithe merely stared at him, thin eyebrows lifted.

Her bed was warm, soft. The coverlets were light,

but they made a nest for his huge body and he slept without dreaming, but then in the night a red light made him open sleepy eyes and by the reflection of the fireflames in the greystone hearth, he saw Leithe standing, slipping down her black garments, revealing her pallid skin, the heavy breasts and smooth slopes of hips and thighs. She seemed a succubus to the drowsing giant.

Through his lashes he saw her approach the bed, smiling down at his recumbent figure. Her hand caught the coverlets, threw them back. She knelt on the bed, bending down to kiss his lips with a mouth that was fire and velvet.

"As Afgorkon put magic into your steel, so I shall put a little magic in your body, barbarian," she whispered.

Her hand ran down his chest. . . .

Kothar woke to morning sunlight, wondering if he had dreamed last night, when Leithe had stripped off her garments and had come into this bed with him. She was not there now but the pillow beside his own was indented, where a head had lain. A long black hair rested on the pillow.

With a chuckle, Kothar reached for it, tied it on a knot about a lock of his yellow mane. "For luck," he told himself. He felt renewed in his strength and cunning, and wondered idly if there had been any truth in what the sorceress had whispered to him about putting magic in his flesh.

Leithe was nowhere in the tower but there was food on the dining room table, hot and tasty, and outside the tower door a black horse stood, caparisoned in silvered bridle and reins, with an ornate saddle of silver and ivory for his sitting.

Drawing the cloak of Thaladomis about his great shoulders, he kicked the black stallion to a gallop.

Along the narrow, dusty little roads of Nirvalla the iron hooves of the great warhorse carried thunder in a rolling tattoo as its long strides ate up ground. Past a hillside where a small farm lay, leaving a small castle behind on distant hills, the stallion ran on and on.

The twisted ruin of a great tree, its limbs and twigs black against the yellow sky, told Kothar he was near his destination. He drew back on the reins and the horse slowed to a canter. A narrow trail led up into the low hills past the tiny farm buildings. Kothar chose that pathway, letting the stallion walk.

Where a stone fence bordered a field where young lambs browsed, the Cumberian swung out of the saddle. His eyes took in the scene, saw also a small shed that held tools, and he found, upon investigation, a number of sheepskins for the tanning. One of the sheepskins was supple to the touch; Kothar dropped the cloak, tossing the woolly hide about his broad shoulders.

On hands and knees he crept into the meadow and mingled with the lambs. The sight of him did not startle them, they were reassured by the sign of the hide atop his back.

Neither was Skrye surprised, an hour later, for from the air, Kothar looked to be no more than a big ram. Downward from the clouds floated the big eagle, wings widespread as it glided like a ghost, ever earthward. Kothar saw him, grinned coldly, and crept forward like a sheep nibbling the grass.

Skrye floated thirty feet above the flock.

Under his hide, the barbarian sweated. Would the eagle drop near him? Or would it swoop down for a tiny lamb on the fringe of the flock, too far away for him to reach it? He waited with the patience of the animal he so much resembled.

Skrye screeched and fell.

Straight downward he dropped, talons spread wide for a small, woolly back. Kothar grunted gratefully, edged closer.

As those talons closed, Kothar sprang.

His hands went into feathers and across a golden leg. Skrye screamed, startled, turned its head, drove its sharp beak at this oddly shaped sheep. Kothar flinched and cursed as his flesh tore and blood showed but his fingers merely tightened. He rose upward to his feet, and now both hands were about the legs of Skrye as he swung him around and around over his head.

Kothar bent, drove Skrye downward at a big grey rock half-buried in the meadowland loam. The bird bounced when it hit, but it fought back, contorting its body, tearing with its beak at the big gash in Kothar's forearm its first attack had caused.

Three more times Kothar swung the bird. It did no good, and now he realized that the magic of Thaladomis protected it. Perhaps not even steel could harm Skrye.

Ahhh! But he carried more than steel.

Frostfire!

He let go the eagle. Instantly it was up, away. Yet Kothar was whipping out the blue blade of his sword, and in that same movement, cutting upward so that the blade made a blur in the clear air.

The edge slashed into a wing of the rising eagle, it sheared away flesh and feathers. With a cry of stark fury, the bird fluttered weakly to the ground. Kothar was after it, using the point. He jabbed, impaling the eagle, holding it, screaming and still struggling, to the grass.

Skrye took time to die, but when it was dead, Kothar knelt and fumbled until his bloody fingers closed on something ovoid in shape and hard to the touch. He brought it out into the sunlight, and saw that it was the ruby of Warrl. He wiped the jewel and his hands clean on the meadowland dirt, then crossed the fields to where a little trickle of water came along the spillway of the farm springhouse.

He washed the blood and dirt from the ruby and from his hands. He slipped the jewel into a fold of his loincloth and tightened the rope belt that held it.

Then he rode to the black tower.

Leithe washed his badly gashed forearm with soapy water and a soft cloth and spread a salve on the flesh which healed it within the hour. Her lips twitched from time to time at sight of the single black hair knotted into his yellow mane, and her beautiful features assumed a satisfied look.

"Without that strand of my hair, you might have died," she told him, and broke into soft laughter. "Or if I had not come to sleep with you last night, to give your flesh a little of my own magic. I'm glad to see you are a sensible man. Now let me see the ruby."

She took it into her palms, cupping them so the blood-red jewel glinted evilly. Long she looked into its red depths, sighing and nodding her head, before she spoke again.

"Yes, the demon is trapped inside it, where Thaladomis put him," she murmured. "And he begs for freedom. His name is Warrl, and he burns to have revenge on the magician."

"Dare we free him?" Kothar asked, staring at the jewel.

"We must free him, if we ever hope to get the helix back into Nirvalla. The spell that keeps the helix in your world will be broken when Warrl is loosed. But since there will be incantations on the ruby, so that it will not crack like an ordinary jewel, we must make preparations."

In her incantation chamber, Kothar watched Leithe

light the coals and toss certain herbs on them when they glowed red, so that a pungent, pleasant smell rose into the air. From one of the opened volumes, Leithe studied the magic formula that would enable her to set Warrl free.

In a golden mortar, she ground up with a golden pestle the dried hide of a frog, the eyes of a cat, nard and wolfbane, poppy seeds and black water from a witch pool, making a rich paste. Lifting the ruby, she smeared the paste over it.

"Fetch the warhammer, Kothar," she commanded.

From its peg along the wall above a cabinet containing the gall bladder of a dog, the liver of a boar and the other herbs and spices which Leithe employed in her necromancies, the barbarian lifted down the long-handled weapon and Leithe, using a silver mortar and pestle this time, ground up purple foxglove mixed with henbane and the roots of dried Kolor beans with water, forming a purplish liquid. Kothar came at her gesture, dipping the flat end of the warhammer into the mixture.

Leithe placed the ruby on a flat slab. "Strike!" she cried.

Kothar raised the warhammer, brought it down upon the ruby. The jewel cracked to the sound of a thousand bells clanging, and from its red interior, amid the shards of shattered ruby, lifted a blackish smoke.

Leithe made a sign in the air. "Peace between us, Warrl—and peace between you and this warrior."

Red eyes glowed in the midst of the black cloud, and a deep voice said, "Peace between us, Leithe, and with you, warrior. My quarrel is with Thaladomis!"

"Go, Warrl. We have freed you."

"I shall go. My gratitude to you both."

The black smoke whirled, fluttered a moment, and was gone. Kothar let out his breath slowly, aware that the hairs on the back of his neck were stiff, and that his sun-bronzed flesh crawled. He did not like demons or wizards, but they were a necessary part of his world.

Give him the cold wind blowing across the ice wastes and a white bear at bay to his hunting spears, and he was content. Give him a horse beneath him to ride, Frostfire to swing at a human foe, and he was happy.

As for warlocks and their spells—

"Fauggghh!" he growled, shaking himself.

Leithe smiled, put a pale hand on his hairy forearm. "It was necessary, Kothar. Now you can leave Nirvalla, but wear your cloak. Much of the black magic has gone out of the helix, but it is still dangerous to mortal hands. Go now, with my gratitude, and that of Phronolom and Ayatha."

"What of Kyros?"

"He stays here." She shrugged. "He is harmless without his soldiers and Thaladomis, being nothing but a fat little man. Let the naiads keep him for their plaything, if they will. He cannot harm anyone, now."

"And Ayatha? Didn't you say she was in thrall? That she sleeps in her bed like a dead woman?"

"The ruby has been shattered, Warrl freed. Ayatha too, has been freed. She is alive, and in the arms of Phronalom at this very moment."

Kothar grinned, nodding. His big hands hitched at Frostfire, drew his cloak closer about his giant frame. "I'll be gone, then. But—how do I get back?"

Leithe said, "Speak these words, 'krthnol abbatt sorgik.' Ah, and when you take the helix from the galley, say the single word 'horthidol'!"

The barbarian nodded.

As if at a sudden thought, he stepped forward, caught Leithe in his arms, and mashed her lips with his, holding her close in his embrace. He felt a fire in his flesh at the touch of her soft body to his, but this woman was not for him.

He let her go. She laughed happily and whispered the words that he repeated after her.

"Krthnol abbatt sorgik!"

Leithe and her room of incantations was gone.

5

The helix gleamed in golden splendor in front of him.

Kothar saw that the room was bare of the white mists; probably, he reasoned, because the evil emanations of Warrl no longer touched the golden spiral. Kothar put out his hands toward the glistening helix.

"Horthidol," he breathed, and the helix lifted easily into his fingers. Gently he carried it to the window, where he wrapped the cloak about it.

He slid a foot through the cabin window and stepped out into the night. Below him, naked and cold and wet, the Oasian dancing girl shivered to the cold night winds blowing across Lake Lotusine. At sight of him, she gave a glad little cry.

"I was afraid," she panted, reaching up toward him as he came downward, toes and fingergrips supporting his big body. "There have been terrible sounds and cries from the deck."

"There may be even worse ones, soon," he rumbled.

The girl rose up to press herself against him, her hands caressing his shoulders and back while she pressed her lips to his chest. Kothar grinned. Aie! The sorceress Leithe had been every inch a woman, but this dusky daughter of the southlands was all the woman any man might need, and the witchery she possessed had only to do with her beauty and not with spells and incantations.

He kissed her with the savagery of the northlands in his mouth; she moaned and squirmed against him.

"They killed Gorth finally," she told him when he let her go, "and just tossed his body overboard."

"We'd better get away," he growled. "A demon's coming for Thaladomis—and I don't want to be around when they meet. By Dwallka! I've had my belly full of magic for the nonce."

But he was too late.

Already an eerie wail was rising from the deck. Kothar caught the girl to him, shifting her onto his broad back where she locked legs about his middle and arms about his neck for easier riding. She caught the cloak-wrapped helix in a hand so he could use both arms for climbing.

"I'll take one look," he rasped.

He went up the side of the gilded galley as a monkey might run up a treebranch in the vast jungles south of Ispahan. His head lifted above the rail, followed by her own.

A dark smoke was writhing on the galley deck. To one side of it a noblewoman, dark of hair and stripped to a tiny girdle during the carousing following the killing of the great bear, shrank back at sight of it. Her eyes bulged, both hands were lifted palms outward as if to halt its progress. Her mouth was contorted in a grimace of stark fear as she made little whimpering sounds.

"No, no—stay away! Whatever you are—stay back!"

At her cry, men turned from the tables set with fruit and meats and cups of fine Salernian wine, where the courtiers of the royal court feasted and made merry in the absence of the emperor. The women who were being disrobed as the night wore on, who perched on laps or leaned against men flushed with wine, were forgotten. And Thaladomis, who sat at the end of the table, waited upon by two rich noblewomen, stark naked, whom it was his amusement to humble and degrade, paused with a fruit halfway to his lips.

As that black cloud grew and took shape, the magician leaped to his feet, scattering a bowl of fruit and a wine-cup. His face was white as the snows of Thuum, there was utter terror in his gaze.

"No!" he screamed. "You are safe in—"

The dark cloud firmed into shape, towering upward into the semblance of a winged man, a man with heavy, rolling muscles and long, furry ears. The blazing red eyes, filled with hate, with the lust to slay, froze every man and woman motionless at that banqueting table.

"I come, Thaladomis! For your mean, arrogant soul I thirst! You shall attend me at *my* banqueting hall— for all eternity! Between the tortures fallen demons suffer, you shall wait on me day and night, without food—what need has a spirit for food?—and without rest from the blows and buffets which shall be your pay in my employ!"

Thaladomis screamed. He alone of all the feasters understood what the demon meant, how he spoke truth, that he reigned in a sub-world out of which Thaladomis had summoned him, to entrap him in the ruby.

The magician could not move. It was as if he had been turned to stone. He watched, as did the others but with greater terror in his soul, as Warrl became massive reality on the deck planks and stepped forward to claim his slave.

His arm went out, lifted Thaladomis into the air.

Gripping the body of the magician in his left fist, Warrl caught his left arm and twisted it savagely. Thaladomis screamed in agony.

"Stop! Stop! You're twisting off my arm!"

"What need has a spirit for arms, mage?"

He ripped loose the arm. As Thaladomis came close to fainting in his agony, Warrl turned his attention to his other arm, turning it, yanking it, until it flew through the air out over the waters of Lake Lotusine.

Behind him, Kothar felt Laella shuddering in horror, whispering, "I cannot look! It is awful. He is a wicked man but—"

"He would have kept Warrl inside the ruby forever," Kothar rumbled. "The demon seeks only just vengeance. And the ways of demons are not our ways. We might show mercy, not a demon!"

A leg fell to the deck. A second leg was flung into the night. Thaladomis was no more than a mewling torso of a man.

In his vast hand, Warrl lifted him high, shook him in the air. "What? Not dead yet? Come, Thaladomis— yield up your spirit to me, or off comes your head, as well!"

"Yes, yes!" cried the wizard. "Anything—to end this agony!"

Something thin and grey fluttered where the armless, legless torso hung in that dark, ebon hand. A shriek, and the torso fell, and now Warrl gripped merely a struggling length of—emptiness—in his fist.

The demon flung back his head, hailed laughter to the sky.

"I win, Thaladomis! You are mine—for all eternity!"

The wind blew across the deck.

A woman wept softly in the night.

The deck was empty where Warrl had stood.

Kothar lowered himself away from the rail. In moments he was dipping his feet and then his body into the cold waters of the lake. He took back the helix in the cloak, and with Laella beside him, struck out for the nearest shore.

The dancing girl kept good time, trailing him by only a little on their way toward the stones of an old quay jutting out from a small dock. Behind the dock was an old warehouse, its doors closed at this hour of the morning. Dawn was still an hour away, and soon the cobblestoned streets would know the rattle of cartwheels and the tramp of early risers on their way to work.

Kothar put a hand on a piling, yanked himself upward. He put a hand down, drew the shivering, wet dancing girl up onto the stone to stand beside him. She was naked, but Kothar dared not remove the cloak from about the helix for fear it would blast them both. He himself only wore his wet loincloth and Frostfire in its scabbard. He shifted the belt about his middle to make running that much easier.

"Running will warm you," he told the girl.

Hand in hand they sped away across the cobblestones.

They met no one on the way to the walled gardens of Nestorius the merchant, and the big stone house flanking it, where a single window glowed golden with light behind its curtain. The barbarian held the shivering Oasian close against him as his hand made thunder with the knocker.

To his surprise, the street door was opened almost immediately. The same girl who had opened it when Rufflod stood beside him smiled at him and looked with surprise at the naked Laella.

"I'll fetch clothes," she said, and fled.

Moments later, the Oasian dancing girl was slipping into a woolen kirtle that came to the middle of her thighs. Her feet went into sandals, and then she stood and shook back her long black hair, letting it dry in the wind sweeping across the garden. Kothar put on a dry loincloth, a fur kilt, and a heavy woolen shirt.

"Nestorius is awake," the girl said. "He waits for you."

She brought them across the garden and into the big stone house. The night was very still around them, the flapping of the girl's sandals were loud in the otherwise-silent house.

Nestorius was standing in his library, tall and saturnine, his dark face flushed with expectancy. His eyes went at once to the helix wrapped inside the cloak and he put his hands together, rubbing them.

"You have it," he cried, and there was both surprise and excitement in his voice. "I never thought you could do it, despite what Rufflod said. Where is he, by the way?"

"Dead," answered Kothar. "The helix killed him—as it will kill you if you stand in the same room with it, while not wearing this cloak. Let the cloak dry, put it on—and you can step into a strange world beyond our own."

He told of his adventure while Nestorius listened.

When he was finished, the merchant said, "Then I have sent you on a fool's errand. What good is the helix to me, if this Phronalom may send a demon to take it back?"

The barbarian shrugged. "I brought you the helix, that was our agreement. I made no promises as to what the helix was, what treasure it might bring you. That was your concern."

Nestorius smiled coldly. "I pay for services, barbarian. Why should I pay you good gold for something I won't be able to keep?"

Kothar put out his hands and closed them on the fur-trimmed cotehardie the merchant wore. Easily he lifted the man into the air, shaking him gently.

"Nestorius, I like not your cheating ways. I would as soon kill you as let you trick me out of my money. Now hand over the leather bag with the gold and the jewels in it that I earned this night, by Dwallka!"

The trader read the hard blue eyes of the Cumberian correctly and sweat came out upon his brow. "Let me down," he cried, "or I'll have my guards in on you to toss you in one of the emperor's jails."

Kothar grinned. "If you do, you'll be dead before they get here! And the emperor won't be coming back. Now—which is it?"

Nestorius nodded his head, smiling grimly. "Very well. Set me down. I'll give you the gold."

The barbarian lowered him. At the same time, the merchant broke free and leaped toward the shelves that lined his study. His hand went out toward the leather sacks piled there. Instead of lifting a sack, Nestorius put his hand on the bell and yanked it off the shelf.

In a moment the clangor of the bell would alert his guards. Triumph shone in the face of the lean, dark man and a grin revealed his teeth.

Suddenly, the room was cold.

No blast of freezing gale from the ice wastes of Thuum could have been more frigid. Hoarfrost formed instantly on the shelves, the books, the paintings and draperies on the wall. Icicles hung from the ceiling as the moist air froze under that arctic blast.

Nestorius froze too, eyes wide with horror.

A demon writhed into being in the room, white, coated with rime, pink eyes glowing in a face which seemed made from ice. Its pink eyes touched Nestorius, the barbarian and the dancing girl, then settled on the helix in the sodden cloak.

It moved forward, and Kothar heard the sound of ice crunching, a sound he had heard many times when he had stood atop the great glacier of his northern home-lands.

"No!" screamed the merchant, and leaped.

"Stand back!" the ice demon warned.

Nestorius took no heed of that icy voice. He caught the helix in his arms, wrapped them about the cloak-shrouded spiral. "It's mine," he panted. "I paid good gold for its delivery. That makes it mine!"

"It belongs to Phronalom, it is not yours."

"Besides, you paid no gold," Kothar grated. "You denied your debt, which means the helix does not belong to you—but to me, the thief who took it. And I give it away freely."

Nestorius stared from the man to the demon. "I will pay. I was but jesting. Take the leather sack—take two!"

Inexorably the demon moved on the merchant who went back two steps, then three, until the draperied wall permitted him to go no farther. The ice-being advanced, white arms held out. Its frigid fingers it placed on Nestorius.

The merchant stiffened. Hoarfrost covered his cote-hardie, his body; icicles formed on his face. He was dead, frozen, propped up against the wall.

The demon took the helix and the cloak away from his nerveless fingers. For a moment he stared down at it. Then he was gone.

Laella shook herself, pushing back her long hair. "Gods of Oasia—I'm freezing! Kothar—let's get out of here!"

The barbarian stared at the rigid body of the mer-chant, nodding. "Yes. I don't want to be blamed for Nestorius' death."

Laella ran to the shelf, snatched at two leather bags fat with coins and jewels. "I'll take these to pay for all the trouble you've been through. We both deserve something, and Nestorius has no further need for gold."

She ran for the door, clutching the bags.

Kothar followed after her, pausing only for one long, last glance at the dead merchant. Strange. If the merchant had played honest, there would have been no trouble. He might still be alive. His greed had been so great that his heart, unable to take the strain of losing the helix, had burst inside his rib cage.

Laella was in the doorway, waving a hand.

"Come, Kothar! We can buy passage to the south-lands with but a small part of all this gold."

He ran after the girl, wondering how long he would be permitted to keep the gold and the jewels. The girl, now, was another matter. It would be a long trip to Oasia. The nights would be dark velvet and the girl warm and fragrant in his arms.

Kothar grinned and ran the faster.

A PLAGUE OF DEMONS

1

For three days, on the long ride from Romm to Clon Mell in the land of Gwyn Caer, Kothar the barbarian had seen the face of Red Lori, and heard her threats.

The first time she appeared to his eyes, he was making a campfire on the border region between the misty swamp and the lands of the baron lords. There was the smell of salt in the air from the dying sea that had beat against the shore of what was now Avalonia, eons ago. Cattails swayed to the cool wind whipping the swamp waters into tiny ripples. Laella was off gathering twigs and he was alone with the red flames his flint and steel had sparked.

Red Lori was a part of those flames, laughing up at him, her slanted green eyes narrowed, her red tongue showing between her teeth.

"Two days, barbarian. Two days of life remain!"

She was lovely, Kothar thought, staring at her image in the fire. Too bad she was a witch—or had been, before Kothar had hung her in a silver cage in the palace of Queen Elfa of Commoral—for she was a disturbingly beautiful woman. Long red hair fell to her curving white haunches, and her breasts were full and tilted. Naked she stood in her cage, naked she appeared to him now.

Then she was gone; only her taunting laughter remained.

The second time she appeared was as he bent above a pool inside the mountain barriers of Gwyn Caer, hands cupped to lift cool mountain water to his lips. The Oasian dancing girl was changing her garments behind a stand of pines that protected her from the cold boreal breezes. The witch-woman stood on the bottom stones, a tiny figurine with arms upraised to him, eyes flaring.

"One day of life is yours, Kothar! Only one remains!"

Then she faded from view, and Kothar drank the water in his cupped hands with a worried scowl on his craggy features. Well he knew and understood the hate of the redhead, he was aware of her ability to talk to demons even if most of her necromantic powers had been stripped from her by the wizard Kazazael before she had been imprisoned in the cage. Still, the demons might obey her and send their dread familiars to slay him to satisfy her need for vengeance.

And then, last night in the Inn of the Cross and Keys within Clon Mell itself, within range of the bells that rang like sweet music from church spires and temple cloisters, she had come again. Laella sat across the wooden tabletop from him in a woolen tunic hung with chains, her red mouth babbling comments on the people around them, and there was the smell of roasting meat and midlands ale in the air.

He was lifting the leather jack that held his own ale, tilting it to drain the last remaining mouthful, when she was there, a tiny imp inside the leather, up to her knees in cool liquid.

"No day remains! You die this night, Kothar!"

Her laughter rang in his ears.

He marveled that Laella did not hear it, but she was too intent on the dancing girl who had stepped out on a cleared section of the floor, to pay other sights and sounds any attention. The dancing girl was from Makkadonia, dark of skin, with long black hair swaying to her movements. A girdle of coins ringed her bare middle, strings of bells fell from that girdle almost to her ankles. A pair of castanets between her fingers kept rhythm to the jangle of the bells and to the strings and drums of the musicians in a small alcove.

Laella would criticize the dancer, he was sure. She herself had danced, in those days when she had been a slave, before kings and emperors, and would find easy fault with some tavern belly dancer. The barbarian turned his eyes to his leathern jack.

To his surprise, Red Lori was still there.

"Beg me, Kothar! Beg for your life!"

"Not me," he growled.

"Then you die!"

He grinned down at the tiny figure. "Do you think to frighten me?" he jeered. His hand raised the jack, he swallowed the ale, half-expecting to find the woman in his mouth.

She was still inside the jack when he lowered it, laughing up at him. "Then I'll kill Laella! I'll kill both of you!"

"You're afraid," he said suddenly. "That's why you threaten me. Either that—or you have a plan. And Laella doesn't play a part in it. You want her out of the way."

The witch-woman was silent, glaring up at him.

When he put his eyes on the Oasian dancing girl, he saw she was still raptly eying the belly dancer, but with a shade less interest. Red Lori said, "Oh, she can't hear us, she just sees you gawking into your empty ale-mug, like the barbarian boor you are. You're free to talk."

Kothar shook his head. "I won't get rid of her, just to pleasure you. I enjoy her company."

"Then die! I'll be well rid of you."

She faded from view, making an angry gesture.

Kothar sighed and turned in his chair, hand upraised to signal a passing serving wench to come and fill his jack. To Dwallka with Red Lori! He would feast and drink and later he would bed down his Oasian dancing girl in a soft bed in the upper room he had rented that afternoon. The ale and the wanton wisdoms of the Oasian would make him forget the witch-woman and her threats.

Let Red Lori strike—if she could!

2

They came in the dark of the night, three killers from the thieves' market section of Clon Mell, daggers in their hands. They moved as their shadows moved, silently, yet their feet made little sounds where they trampled down the rushes covering the floor of the little bedroom.

Only the animal senses of the big Cumberian saved his life, and that of the Oasian dancing girl curled up against him between the soft sheets. Kothar had been trained to sleep since boyhood with his ears alive to strange sounds. As those rushes crackled ever so faintly, he was off the bed and rolling with Laella in the grip of an arm, flinging the bedsheets behind him to distract their attackers.

His eyes were not bleary from sleep. He saw the dark shapes of the trio of killers, clearly enough, and remembered the threats of Red Lori. The bedsheets he had flung at them entangled their heads. Kothar dove over the bed at them without thinking, putting his hands on the bed, kicking out with his bare feet at the belly of the third man, doubling him up in pain.

Kothar reached out, grabbed the sheeted heads of the other two assassins and rammed their skulls together so hard Laella could hear the sound of their splitting, like overripe melons dropped on a paving-stone. The men sagged, and Kothar let them go, grinning so that he showed his white teeth in his sun-bronzed face like pearls in dark sand as he reached for his great sword.

The blade came free just in time. The man he had kicked in the belly was on top of him, swinging a slim scimitar. Kothar got his sword up just in time, the steel blades rang with a sharp clangor. Then, with a movement so fast Laella could not follow it, Kothar slashed sideways with the keen edge of Frostfire.

Through flesh and blood he drove his steel, cleaving deep into the assassin who stood a moment, mouth open, eyes wide, before he realized that his body had been cut almost in half. He made a mewling sound, then was silent as he died.

Over the bed and the three dead bodies, Kothar stared at the naked girl. "They might have killed you," he told her.

"They didn't," she pointed out.

He lifted the sheet that covered the two dead men and wiped his blade on it, very carefully. His face was twisted in thought, and then he shook his head.

"If they had killed me, they wouldn't have let you live. I can't let you die, Laella. I've got to send you home to your people."

She argued all the rest of the night but the barbarian would not listen to her. "Enough that you were almost killed! Another time, I might not hear them as they came."

"Why did they try to kill you?"

His brawny shoulders lifted in a casual shrug. "Who knows? Maybe Kyros' uncle sent them, for having done away with the emperor."

He did not tell her about Red Lori.

Early next morning, the chiming of camel bells made sweet sounds in the air as they walked through the merchant bazaar toward the stalls where Althassar the Miser was forming a trade caravan for the southern lands. Kothar strode along with a black scowl on his face, Laella with the traces of tears recently dried.

To Althassar the Miser he growled, "I'm sending her back to her folks. She's too much for me. She drains me with her embraces."

Well, Laella thought, it's as good an excuse as any.

The bearded merchant grinned knowingly while Kothar poured out gold pieces from his leather sack. He was about to make a quip about barbarians and Oasian girls but the hard face of the youthful giant before him made him bite his tongue.

Kothar was not happy about this parting. He would miss the dancing girl, but he was determined that Red Lori would not get the chance to strike at him through her.

Ah, well. A lonely campfire and life was preferable to a soft bed and loving female flesh, when a dagger-stab might come with it.

It had been a pleasant interlude.

Now it was over.

Kothar took the girl into his arms for a farewell kiss. She wriggled her soft flesh against him in a desperate attempt to remind him of what he would be missing, once she mounted her camel and became part of the caravan being formed by the bearded merchant.

Then he pushed her away, and strode off between a pile of Vandacian carpets displayed by two old men. Kothar walked swiftly, not looking back. He would miss the girl. By the gods, he would! She had made a most pleasant traveling companion.

It was for her own good, this parting.

But—was it?

Kothar admitted he felt a sense of freedom he had not known since he had taken up with the Oasian wench. He could go where he would now, without worrying about finding a bed to sleep in and a wooden tabletop off which to eat. He could hunker down beside a twig fire and cook his meal and eat it, and let the wind blow free about his fur-clad shoulders.

He walked purposefully through the bazaar, his mind on the little shop of the trader Pahk Mah. Pahk Mah dealt in silver and strange weapons, in gold wares and in the spices of the Orient, in slavegirls and in jewels. He asked no questions of the men who brought him curiously carved little statues or jewels that might have been taken from the rings women wore, for Pahk Mah was known to the brotherhood of thievery as a fence.

Not that the jewels in his little leather bag were stolen, Kothar reasoned, though Laella had snatched them without permission. It was just caution that made him turn into the little cobblestoned street at the end of which the shop of Pahk Mah made itself known by a wooden sign hanging on iron chains above its recessed doorway.

His hand pushed the door, but it would not open. Kothar peered in through the grimy glass, seeing ivory statuettes of naked women in lewd poses, candlesticks carved from solid gold, ebony trays and bowls, ivory canisters, weapons fashioned by the ironworkers of Abathor who were reputedly among the finest ever known.

The interior of the shop was a hodgepodge of miscellany.

It was also empty.

With the flat of his hand, the barbarian pounded on the door. "Pahk Mah!" he bellowed. "Pahk Mah! Open up."

He saw movement in the dark recesses of the shop, near the long wooden counter, where rare books on demonolotry and necromancy sat binding by binding alongside ceremonial bells and incensories in which the

forbidden scents of Ikrikone might be burned by initi-
ates to the dark rites.

His hand beckoned. The figure in the shadows
scurried forward. When he passed a beam of dying
sunlight, Kothar recognized the man for Ishral, the
assistant to Pahk Mah. Ishral made flapping motions
with his hands, indicating that the barbarian should go
away.

Kothar grinned, lifting out the leather sack and shaking it. He even poured a couple of the jewels onto his
palm where they sparkled as if with inner fires.

Ishral came close to the door.

"Go away. The old man is ill."

"Then somebody must have cheated him in a trade.
The old man hasn't known a day of sickness in his life.
Now let me in, Ishral, or I'll kick down your door and
all the thieves in Clon Mell will be here within seconds
to loot and steal."

Ishral shook his head, but his hands went to the
latches and the bolts behind which Pahk Mah barricad-
ed himself. As the door opened, his quavering voice
protested, "He will beat me for this. I ought to have my
head examined."

The Cumberian clapped his bony shoulder with a
hand. "I bring rare jewels to the old man, jewels he will
be delighted to see."

Ishral shuffled ahead of him, grumbling denials. He
was even older than Pahk Mah, Kothar thought, following him. Men said Ishral had been a slave, long
ago, who had made love to a queen of Aegypton and
had been caught in the process by a jealous lover. As a
result, Ishral had lost that which made him a man.

It was probably just gossip, but the man did speak in
a high voice, and he had no use for women, as far as
anyone knew. He was bald, with a forked beard and
piercing black eyes, and his skin was a fishbelly white.

Altogether, an unlovely specimen, but he was shrewd, as grasping and as clever as Pahk Mah, and there were some who claimed he was a partner to the shopkeeper.

Ishral paused at a leather curtain.

"Wait here, I will tell the old one," he said.

"Nonsense, he'll be glad to see me," Kothar grinned, and swept aside the hanging. He paused, honestly shocked.

An old man Pahk Mah was, he knew. But this bag of bones who sat hunched on a stool before this back-room fireplace, thin and with white hair, eyes rheumy and shivering steadily, was something more than old. This man was absolutely terrified.

The barbarian strode forward.

He felt the warmth of the flames on his booted legs, and his brawny body made a shadow that fell across the bent, shivering figure.

"What's wrong, old friend?" he asked quietly.

"I am cursed by the gods," the old man wailed.

"Nonsense. What gods there are only exist in the minds of men. Now speak out, tell me what's bothering you."

"It's my daughter, Mahla."

"Pretty little Mahla of the gold hair? Has she died?"

"Not yet. She dies tonight!"

Kothar reached for a three-legged stool, dragging it forward and settling his rump on it, frowning. He remembered Mahla from the last time he had been in this shop. She had been little more than a child, slimly curved but with a sweet face and long yellow hair that fell to her hips.

"Who kills her, old one?"

"The worshipers of the dark god, Pulthoom. They celebrate his rites in the ruins of the old abbey outside the city, where the old city used to be before it was razed because of the magicks performed within its walls."

Kothar growled, "I'll save her. I'll go at once."

The old man shook his head, staring blindly into the fire. "It's no use. I offended the priests of Pulthoom by not giving them a sacred golden bowl my agents found in the ruins of Allakar. For nothing! They wanted it for nothing!"

Pahk Mah turned his head and stared hard at Kothar. His eyes were suddenly bright and keen, hard as agates. The hair on his head was white, but his face was carefully shaved. He had been a tall, powerful man once. Now he seemed wasted away.

"You can do nothing, Kothar," he said softly. "I have offended Pulthoom and I will be punished. So say his priests. They took Mahla away with them, as evidence of what my punishment shall be. They intend to sacrifice her this night at Thistern Abbey."

"They have to wait for darkness. It isn't dark yet."

"I thank you for your intentions, but you can do nothing against a god. I have sinned, I shall be punished."

"Why didn't you give them the bowl?"

The old man snarled, "What? And lose money?"

"Isn't your girl worth more than money?"

"Yes, but at the time, I didn't know what the priests would do. After they took Mahla, I offered them the bowl, but they said I must pay for my sins. My dearest treasure—my Mahla—must die, they said. Only in such a way would I understand the power of the dark god."

"Hogwash," growled the barbarian. They were just taking advantage of an old man. Besides, they needed a living sacrifice to Pulthoom and only a female would do.

His hand hitched Frostfire between his legs.

He held no love for the priests of these dark gods.

They were cunning, cruel men, for the most part, and they used Pulthoom and his godhood as excuses to take what they wanted in the way of wealth or womanhood.

Kothar doubted that they would kill Mahla. More likely they would throw a scare into her and keep her as a plaything for their lusts. After they tired of her, they could always stick a dagger between her ribs.

"Pahk Mah, let me leave this with you for study."

Kothar handed over the leather sack.

The old man came to life, nodding and undoing the pull cord, letting the jewels roll out on his palm. His eyes blazed, he made a little sound with his lips.

"They are excellent gems, they have been selected for size and color by an expert. I'm not going to ask where they come from, enough for me that they'll be mine." Placing the jewels back into the sack, Pahk Mah pulled tight the strings.

"Now tell me, what do you want in exchange for them? Money, I suppose. All you wanderers are the same."

Kothar smiled grimly. "I don't know what I want, as yet. I'll know more about that, after I get your girl back."

Pahk Mah opened his eyes wide. "You'd dare do that? Leap in among the worshipers of the dark god and grab her?"

"If it means I'd get you to judge my jewels and give me fair recompense for them, I would. I can't have you sitting here moping away your days. I need money for my travels. If this is the only way to get it, I'll do it."

He rose to his feet, towering above the old man. In his fur jerkin and mail shirt, he made a giant figure, his bared arms bulging with muscle, his legs naked between his kilt and his warboots.

"How do I find this abbey?" he asked.

It was Ishral who answered, from the leather drape

where he had been standing. "You follow the Street of the Silk Sellers down a slope and then out across the heath. You can scarcely miss them. The ruins are the only things on the heath."

The man turned and walked away, letting the leather curtain rustle into place. Kothar went after him, turning once to study the old man who was shaking the jewels out of the little leather sack and studying them. The barbarian nodded, apparently satisfied.

From the old man, his eyes went casually to a length of wrapping out of which protruded a length of obal horn. Intrigued, the barbarian stepped closer, gripping the wrapping and throwing it back.

"What's this? I never knew Pahk Mah to treasure anything so much that he wrapped it up like a babe in swaddling clothes."

The wrapping came undone. Before him lay a horn bow perhaps five feet in length, polished and gleaming as if new. Beside it lay a quiver, filled with arrows.

"By Dwallka! No wonder he cares for it so tenderly. This is a weapon fit for a king. Here, let me test it."

Ishral mumbled, "It was the bow of Krangor of Abathor, he who lived two centuries ago and carved out a kingdom for himself in the southlands."

Kothar grinned, "Stolen, no doubt, from the temple where it rested by some quick-fingering thief. I'll take it as part payment for those jewels."

Ishral shrugged.

With the bow in a hand, with the quiver over a shoulder, the barbarian strode out into the dying sunlight. Behind him, he heard the bolts and latches click into place.

Outside the shop, the wind had sprung up. It ruffled the fur of his jerkin and swung the wooden shop-sign on its iron chains. Here and there a man hurried along, head bent. The sky was darkening, the cool chill of coming night was already in the air.

Kothar walked the Street of the Silk Sellers like a lion padding along a jungle trail, not noticing the glances his giant bulk received, intent only on finding Thistern Abbey and rescuing the girl who would be flat on her back on the sacrificial stone.

It would not be an easy task, her rescue. The worshipers of the dark god were fanatics, half-crazy men who would not think twice about sticking a dagger in his back, even as he made his escape from the ruins. Kothar grinned at his thoughts. By Dwallka, he was no fat southlander to accept cold steel gracefully! He would kill first, laying about him with Frostfire until he cleared a path for himself and little Mahla.

And yet, he could not run forever with Mahla in his arms, not with the hue and cry after him. He would need horses. He had stabled his warhorse Greyling and the white mare on which he and Laella had ridden into Clon Mell, at a blacksmith shop not far from here. It would be best to make a small detour, and get them.

He paid over two copper coins to the smith and swung up into the kak. Holding the reins of the smaller horse, which had belonged to Laella, he moved eastward toward the vast stretch of heath.

He did not see the man Ishral, who had come to a street well and paused there, watching Kothar as he cantered away from the Street of Silk Sellers. Under the grey hood of his cloak, that he wore against the gathering wind, Ishral was smiling grimly.

Kothar would not live to see the rites of Pulthoom.

3

The heath stretched like a corner of fabled Aedenn across the world. Overhead the stars were flicking into life in a grey bowl of sky, and where the bluebells and the heather stretched their petals, the wind moaned and whistled as if to announce the coming of the dark god.

Kothar rode with his head bowed, aware that on such a night as this, Pulthoom the Black Lord would find it easy to penetrate the barriers between worlds and make his dread presence known. Kothar had no doubt of his ability to steal Mahla from the frenzied worshipers, but the dark god himself was another matter. He did not like to fight with gods or demons.

He could see nothing but the vast wasteland on either side of him. Due to the gathering dusk, the spires and rooftops of Clon Mell were nothing but a haze on his back trail. He felt alone, but this fact could not account for the coldness rippling up and down his spine.

Kothar had been alone too often for that.

No, this uneasiness was the result of that animal instinct which was so much a part of him. As might the wary wolf near a trap, Kothar sensed danger.

He did not shift position, he kept Greyling to a steady walk. But under his hood his eyes raked the heath in front of him. No need to look upon his back trail, his ears would hear the sound of hooves galloping, if there was danger behind him.

What danger there might be was in front of him.

He was nearing a group of jagged rocks, jutting upward from the heath floor like the gnarled fingers of some half-buried giant. A man or two might hide among those rocks, very easily.

Kothar reined in the roan.

He reached downward blindly, his fingers fumbling for the horn bow he had taken from among the weapons in the shop of Pahk Mah. Its tip he put on his foot in an iron stirrup. His muscles rolled, bulging, as he bent that length of obal horn, bringing its catgut string up over the rock and setting it in place.

His fingers touched the feathered shafts hanging in the hide quiver, lifting one out and nocking it to the bowstring. His laughter rode the wind as he tightened his grip on the bow.

He would not walk blindly into any trap.

The dark worshipers might well post guards to keep the soldiers of the king from harrying them. They might consider Kothar such a warrior. If so, he did not intend to make a sitting target for them.

He slid from the saddle.

He walked across the heath, still wrapped in his cloak, but he had brushed the flaps of that cloak back to free his arms for the firing. His angle of walk would carry him to one side of the rocks.

It was dusk, so he almost missed seeing the touch of black cloth against the grey rock. Only his keen barbarian eyes, trained since birth to see sudden movement, could have picked out that betraying color.

He crouched lower so that the tall grasses hid his huge bulk. Bow in hand, arrow to the string, he sidled forward. The night was still around him, there was no cry of bird or beast, only the faint slither of his warboots on the grass told of his movements.

A man in the black and red robes of a priest of

Pulthoom rose upward. His hands whirled. A *something* flew through the air at Kothar. The big barbarian could not see it clearly, it was too dark.

The horn bow bent. An arrow flew faster than the wind.

The priest in the ornate robes stiffened, jerked. His head whipped back as the arrowshaft buried itself in his chest.

The *something* burst into flames, fifty feet from the barbarian. Kothar stared, slightly awed. What had destroyed that thing? He had not done it, and his animal instinct told him the priest who flung it had not intended his weapon to be destroyed before it reached its target.

The Cumberian ran forward. In the high grasses, he saw a burning length of rope with two round stones attached to each end. Kothar had never seen a bolar before, but he knew the hunters of Gwyn Caer used these weapons to hunt down the long-necked deer that sometimes ran upon the heath.

Bending closer, he saw a face inside the flames.

I destroyed the bolar, Kothar! I have another fate in store for you!

"Your killers failed in the inn bedroom, Red Lori!"

They were not sent to kill, but to warn you! I wanted you to rid yourself of the dancing girl! Where you are going—there shall be women enough for you to handle!

Mocking laughter made the hairs on his neck bristle.

Then—Red Lori was gone.

He stood with the wind howling about him, frowning. His eyes raked the heath, the jutting rock pile. A dead priest lay on those rocks. Did he have a companion? The barbarian moved forward, still alert, yet somehow relaxed. If Red Lori were protecting him, she would let no harm befall him until it was her whim to strike.

Yet he did not abandon his caution. He came upon the rocks from the side, seeing the dead priest with his shaft in his chest lying huddled on the stones. There was no one else in this hiding place.

Kothar bent, yanked out his arrow. These handmade shafts were too valuable to leave lying about. He cleansed the arrowhead in the dirt between the stones while his eyes considered the dead bulk of the priest.

Then his hands were out, stripped off the priestly cloak. Shrugging out of his own grey chlamys he draped it across the dead body. The red and black robe he tossed about his own shoulders. It would be a disguise, of sorts.

He ran down his two horses, mounted Greyling and catching up the reins of the white mare, brought them at a walk toward the abbey ruins.

A red light shone where Thirsten Abbey stood. A sound of voices raised in song came faintly with the wind. The worshipers of the dark god were beginning their evil rites. Where that red light made the darkest shadows Kothar dismounted and tethered the reins to a granite column that leaned sideways against another.

Kothar studied the ancient ruins. Here had been the almonry, yonder the rest rooms for the pilgrims and poorer folk. Behind these had stood the courtyard, that glimmered now in the dim moonlight shining through low, scudding clouds. Grass had grown between the paving stones, and an occasional flower nodded its head to the darkness.

On soundless feet, Kothar moved across that courtyard toward the church. Behind what was left of the church walls, through the openings where once had been stained-glass windows, were the red flares of many torches and the believers gathered to adore Pulthoom.

"Hsssst—Aldred! Over here!"

Kothar shifted the direction of his walk toward a

blackness half-hidden in the shadows. A pale face looked up at him from the rim of a cowl.

"Did you kill the barb—ohhh! You aren't Aldred!"

Big hands went out, drove into the grey wool of the cowl, tightening like claws about a corded throat. The man in the woolen cloak gagged and gurgled, swung off his feet and slammed into the stone wall of the cloister.

"Ishral! By Dwallka—so that's where the treachery lies!"

Kothar released his hold on Ishral to let him speak. When he could, it was with a croak that told how painful it was to drag air into his lungs. "I—I thought to have you killed!

"You went roundabout so as not to be seen while I galloped here as fast as I could! May the dark god claw out your vitals—"

Before he could scream for help, the barbarian swung him up, held his toes inches from the ground while his fingers choked the life silently from the vainly struggling man. A moment later, he let him go. Ishral slumped to the flaggings, lay dead.

Gathering the red and black cloak about him, Kothar stepped forward, moving between two stone abutments that towered overhead. He could see more clearly now by the light of the many torchflames.

On the flat altar where the god Mizran had been worshiped long ago lay the white body of a naked girl. Golden chains held her wrists, golden links her ankles. Bowed before that altar were fifty men and women, keening out their blasphemous hymns. Behind the altar, arrayed in a robe much like that worn by Kothar, stood a priest with a silver bowl raised high. A glittering scythe with a golden handle lay tucked into his white rope belt.

The girl on the altar—could she be Mahla?

Kothar had seen the blonde daughter of old Pahk

Mah more than two years ago. He scowled darkly. She had been a scrawny thing then, with little meat to her bones nor shape to the meat that was there. Yet now she was a woman, it seemed, with finely curved limbs and breasts that formed twin bowls.

She was petrified with fright—or drugs.

She lay with blue eyes wide to the bowl that was being turned by the priest so that a drop of blackish fluid could drip onto her pallid skin, between her breasts. Mahla threw back her head, screeching in agony. Her body strutted its muscles, her legs and arms flailing, causing the golden links of her chains to jangle.

The worshipers raised their heads, their song growing louder as if to drown her cries.

"Thy blood accepts her, dark Pulthoom!" droned the priest.

"Glory to thee, great god," intoned the worshipers.

"Appear before us, feast upon thy gift."

"And do honor to us who worship thee."

They were too intent upon what was happening to the girl to heed the shadowy figure that moved between their kneeling ranks like a panther creeping through veldt grasses. Kothar had seen with a single raking glance that these were no warriors gathered here but fat merchants and lean traders, with their serving maids or shop assistants, pretty girls who were being kept, no doubt, by the same monies they helped earn at their tasks.

Another drop spilled, and again Mahla screamed.

There was a rustling as the woolen paenulas slid down from the heads and shoulders of the men and women. Kothar chuckled, suddenly. Except for those heavy woolen cloaks, everyone was naked.

Kothar held no sympathy for demons. He did not enjoy the supernatural manifestations of the eldritch beings who inhabited his world from time to time. Nor did he relish the spells and incantations of the wizards and sorcerers who summoned up those fiends out of Hel.

He knew that they maintained a grip on their followers by reason of the orgies which followed every rite, being an integral part of it. When female flesh was offered to male flesh to be enjoyed, there were few men who could resist its lure, no matter what its trappings.

The merchants and the traders were here with their pretty assistants to break the humdrum routine of their daily lives. Forgotten were their wives, snugly asleep in their beds. This was a night for revelry.

With complete confidence in his rolling muscles, with an awareness that his only opposition would come from the high priest with the bowl in his hands and the two acolyte priests behind him who led the obscene chantings, Kothar stepped forward.

Sensing his presence, the high priest raised his eyes.

A look of absolute horror made those dark orbs bulge. The worshipers were standing now, their cloaks pooled at their feet. Each man and each woman was naked, ready for the orgiastic rites with which his worshipers greeted Pulthoom. Against this nudity the cloaked figure of the giant barbarian stood out boldly.

"Blasphemer!" screeched the priest.

He drew back the bowl to hurl it.

Kothar leaped. The horn bow went out, hit the bowl, tilting it as horn rang against silver. That dread fluid gushed from the bowl, splattered across the face and throat of the high priest.

His scream was shrill, agonized.

The two other priests leaped forward, sharpened scythes drawn. Kothar rasped a curse, put a palm on the altar and leaped, slashing sideways with the horn. The hard horn hit their faces, drawing blood, as the barbarian drove both feet against the chest of the closest acolyte.

A wail of horror and awe broke from the naked worshipers.

Kothar landed catlike on his feet, the fallen priest on the broken sanctuary floor. Beyond the altar and the priests, a blackness was gathering in the sanctuary, a rolling darkness that sent a stab of abysmal terror into the huge blond barbarian.

Instinctively he dropped the bow, reached for Frostfire.

Red eyes glared down at him from that blackness, at the blasphemer who dared to interrupt these wicked rites. For a few seconds, Kothar crouched frozen, hardly breathing, aware only of his heart hammering away inside his rib cage.

Hate glared at him, and dire threat.

Slowly, then, the blackness dimmed, the red eyes grew pale and lifeless. A wind blew across the sanctuary and the blackness wisped into nothingness. The rites of Pulthoom had been interrupted too soon for the dark god to maintain life in this world.

Kothar came out of his trance in time to see the second acolyte leaping at him with his keen scythe raised high. His arm lifted, drove Frostfire forward, full into the throat of the priest.

Blood spurted. His knees bent, the priest fell.

Kothar swung about, blood dripping from his sword. The naked men and women glared at him but they were unarmed, even had they been willing to stand against this shaggy giant. The barbarian whirled his sword so that the blood-drops flew.

"Begone!" he bellowed. "Lest I slay more than the priests of Pulthoom. This girl—is mine!"

As one, they bent to retrieve their woolen cloaks. They babbled helplessly to one another, from time to time casting their eyes at the naked girl and at the barbarian who meant to take her. They fled when they saw the hard, rocklike bronzed face and the cold blue eyes watching their every move.

When he stood alone in front of the altar, Kothar stooped, fumbled in the belt purse beneath the robes of the high priest, found a little golden key. With the key he unlocked the manacles holding Mahla's wrists and arms ankles.

She moaned, head moving left and right.

"Poor thing," he breathed, bending to lift her.

She opened her long-lashed eyes.

Kothar halted, frozen. There was a glee in those eyes, a wickedness that touched a chord of loathing deep inside him. These were not the eyes of Mahla!

And yet—this was her body!

"Greetings, barbarian," she breathed. "My thanks for rescue."

"Who are you?" he whispered.

She shrugged, lying shamelessly in front of him on the altar top, making no move to rise. "What does it matter? I am Mahla, if you must have a name."

"Not you!" he snorted.

Her laughter rang out, lewd and evil.

"No, you are right. Though this is her flesh, her spirit wanders in the cold grey wastes of Nifferheim. Ah, you start! You know Nifferheim, then?"

In the northland, Nifferheim was that limbo where the spirits of those whose bodies had been displaced by spirits were doomed to wander eternally. If they did not return to their bodies within a certain time, they must spend all eternity in the grey spirit world.

"I see you do," she mocked, lifting a hand. "Here, help me."

Almost unconsciously, his big brown hand went to her small, white fingers, aiding her to sit up. He was staring at her with new eyes, discovering that the sweet lines which had been the face of Mahla were altering subtly. The cheeks were not so full, the eyes seemed slanted, the mouth more boldly curved.

And her body!

Where before Mahla had boasted the clean virginal lines of a girl upon the threshold of womanhood, now her breasts were fuller, heavier, the lines of her hips more rounded. The girlish legs were meatier, more shapely. This was a woman who sat before him naked on the edge of the altar.

"Who are you?" he growled a second time.

"Ahrima. I am a female demon."

His puzzled frown made her smile. "Why does a female demon concern herself with the rites to Pulthoom, you are wondering? Because I was asked to do so, I was promised a reward to take over this body of little Mahla."

She slid off the stone altar and danced a few steps, here and there, her taunting eyes never leaving the scowling face of the big barbarian. She was temptation incarnate in her evil nudity, and that part of him that is in every man was responding to her shameless allure.

"Who?" he blurted, to take his mind off her flesh.

"Red Lori," she laughed, and dancing up to him, threw her arms about his neck. She kissed him hungrily and despite his iron will, Kothar felt the reins of his control slipping badly.

He put his hands to her bare sides to push her away and found himself caressing her soft flesh instead. Against her mouth he muttered, "What does that witch want now?"

"Freedom, Kothar!" cried Ahrima, leaning back to stare up into his face. "And you shall be the man to free her."

"Not me," he grated. "You've wasted your time."

"Have I? What of Mahla who wanders in Niffer-heim? Will you let her stroll eternally in that terrible grey wasteland?"

"What do you mean?" he asked hoarsely.

"When you free Red Lori, I shall go back to my own spirit realm, and the true Mahla shall return into her body. It's that easy to understand, barbarian. Now fetch me a cloak—by the ten eyes of Beeltheer, that wind is cold!"

Her palm chafed her arm as she moved inside the red and black cloak he wore, gathering its flaps about her nudity. She cuddled closer to his big body, her blue eyes gleeful as they stared upward.

"You may be used to these boreal blasts, but I'm a girl demon, and ordinarily I don't feel things like cold and heat. Damn Red Lori, to have induced me to take this task! When I put on human flesh, when I take over a living body, I feel with all their senses."

Kothar pushed her back, reached down and yanked free the rich robes of the high priest. He threw them about her with a snarl. "Here, take this cloak—it goes well with your demon spirit."

She held up a bare foot, smudged with dirt from the altar paving-stones. "And boots for my feet?"

One of the acolytes had feet small enough to possess boots that fit her, he discovered as he knelt to put them on. She stood above him, regal and evil, her brooding eyes and wicked smile acknowledging the fact that she boasted powers that could make this man her slave.

"I am almost jealous of Red Lori, you know," she said softly, wriggling her bare toes to make it harder for him to slip on the second boot. "You might be fun to annoy, to work up into a mad rage upon occasion."

His powerful hands wedged the boot on, making her wince. He growled, "I serve no woman."

"Foolish man," she laughed. "You shall learn."

He glared into her eyes, wondering if he might choke her to death and what the powers of a female demon were, inside its human cage. She was lovely, tempting in the very evil that had altered the features of little Mahla. The wind whipped her long yellow hair, the red torchlights made intriguing shadows on her full red lips.

It took all his will power to keep from gathering her into his arms and crushing her lips with kisses. He was only a man, he thought, and she boasted not only the body of a beautiful woman but the soul of a devil out of Hel.

"You see?" she asked softly.

He shook himself, whirling on a heel and plunging through the night to gather up the reins of the horses. She followed after him, pacing slowly, yet it seemed her footfalls were echoed in his middle.

He held the iron stirrup so she could slide a boot into it and mount into the saddle of the white mare. He felt the touch of her hand on his shoulder as she aided herself to rise.

"You need fear no ambush with me beside you," her voice said above his head. "I am your protection. Now —ride for Commoral!"

He could do nothing else, he decided.

4

Where the high hills of Gwyn Caer merge with the rolling flatlands of eastern Commoral, there is a mountain pass, a narrow trail of worn rock wedged between twin masses of rock and mountainside. It is cold here, the boreal winds blow without ceasing, and the traveler constantly shivers inside his fur-lined clothing.

It was late in the day, the sun was sinking to the west, and the horseman and his female companion found that their tired horses could not carry them as swiftly as they might have wished. Their slow pace annoyed the man, who wanted to reach the lower slopes of these high hills before nightfall.

"You might use a spell to warm the air," he growled, half-turning in his kak to study the woman who rode so gracefully, half the length of a horse behind him.

"I save my spells," she murmured sweetly.

"Why? Let the witch-woman cast her own spells."

"She needs my help. You shall learn why, when the time comes. For now, keep your mount walking. If we must seek night shelter in these wilds, let it be so."

Irritated—what use were female demons if they could not use their demoniac wisdom to aid a man when he needed it? —Kothar swung around to the front. He rode with angry eyes fixed upon the narrow rock path where his stallion walked, and so he did not notice the towering thing that stared down upon him from the stone wall to his right.

It was a furry monster that glared downward with red-rimmed purple eyes, a misshapen thing that resembled a man, but only vaguely, since its body was covered from the top of its skull to its feet with long, white fur.

Few men had ever seen an abominathol, but the tales spun in the alehouses or the way stations that were scattered here and there along this rocky path into Commoral abounded with descriptions of its speed, its fury, its savage destructiveness. Men it tore apart with its huge paws, women it carried off—no man knew where.

It ran lightly on the jagged rocks as it trailed Kothar and Ahrima along the pass. Its eyes gleamed with blood-lust, its breath came shorter, it made little crooning sounds deep in its throat. This night the man would be dead, the woman would be his. And the carcasses of those horses would make good eating.

Dusk came upon the travelers just as the rocks fell away in front of a long stretch of mountain meadow where the snow lay deep. A mile away, Kothar made out the lines of a small hut. Probably the home of a sheepherder, he reasoned, during the milder seasons. It would serve them for the night.

He waved a hand, calling the attention of the woman to the hut. Her eyes studied it carefully, and then she shrugged as if the matter of shelter were of no concern to her. Proud bitch! he told himself silently. She dies from the cold, yet she will not express what she must feel.

"I'll build a fire," he told her. "At least, we won't feel the wind in that place and the flames will warm us. You can do the cooking."

Their saddlebags held food and two bottles of red

Makkadonian wine. It might be pleasant with a fire going and good food in his belly, inside that hut. It would have been pleasant, if Ahrima had not been a demon-woman.

He turned Greyling off the trail and along a narrow footpath, that showed where the snow had sunk a little. Behind the hut was a lean-to, protected from the wind, where he could water and feed the horses.

He came out of the saddle, turning toward the woman. His cupped hands formed a rest for the booted foot she kicked free of the stirrup. She smiled down at him tauntingly.

"Serve me well, Kothar—and I'll plead with Red Lori to let you live for a little while—if only to serve me in my demon world as my slave."

He grunted and turned away, stripping off both saddles, rubbing down the horses, then fitting nosebags on their heads. The grain in the bags would suffice their appetites until they reached the lowlands tomorrow.

Walking into the hut, he found Ahrima huddled in a chair, shivering.

"Why didn't you make a fire?" he rasped.

"I told you, I am saving my powers," she replied, not turning her head to look at him.

He busied himself with the woodpile in the corner, that had been built in the cool days of autumn, setting small, cut logs inside the ring of stone in the middle of the hut. Above this was the funnel of the chimney, opening up wide to absorb the smoke, with a metal spit set into it for the cooking.

Kothar lifted a pair of saddlebags and tossed them at the woman. "If you want to eat, cook!"

Her blue eyes blazed at him. "You can cook for two!"

"I can. I won't," he rasped.

Unfolding a cloth he lifted out a steak and hung it on

a hook above the growing flames. Taking a cooking pot, he went outside, filled it with snow, and brought it back. In moments the smell of cooking steak and boiling kavv filled the little hut.

Ahrima shifted restlessly. Sighing, she unfastened her saddlebags and lifted out her own steak. She nudged him with her shoulder, making him give her room above the flames.

Suddenly the barbarian lifted his head.

"Did you hear that?" he asked, rising to his feet.

Ahrima chuckled. "You're as nervous as a newly captured tiger. Sit down. What is it that you think you're hearing?"

"A footstep outside, crunching snow. Listen!"

Only the wind whistling around the hut touched their ears. Restless, Kothar stalked back and forth. He had taken off his swordbelt for greater ease of movement. Now he strode forward to catch up his blade.

He never reached it.

The wooden wall of the hut bulged inward. Half a dozen planks split. A great arm, covered with long white fur, slid between the openings to catch a plank and rip it loose. An unearthly snarl echoed the sound of splintering wood. Then the abominathol was in the hut, leaping for Kothar.

The big barbarian swung a hamlike fist. It drove into the big-fanged mouth of the beast-man just as Ahrima screamed in horror. The giant Cumberian ducked under a sideswiping paw, drove his other fist under the rib cage of the furry thing. The abominathol roared, reached out both paws and lifted Kothar high.

For a moment it stood on widespread legs, holding the barbarian high. Then it flung him against the far wall. Wood creaked and cracked, dust came out like a mist over Lake Lotusine, and Kothar dropped to the ground.

The abominathol reached for the shrinking Ahrima. "Damned beast," the barbarian snarled, and leaped.

He hit the beast-man, knocked him backward. Fingers locked in the loose fur at its throat, he rode the thing to the hardpacked dirt floor. At the impact of their landing, Kothar lifted upward and banged the abominathol's apelike head down on the ground.

The beast-man howled in mingled pain and fury.

Clawed hands ripped at the Cumberian, tearing the fur of his jerkin but scratching with futile strength on the steel links of his shirt. Kothar drove a fist into the open-mouthed face below him as the abominathol screeched.

It surged upward, carrying the man with it, it caught a pawful of yellow hair and tugged, unbalancing the man and hurling him sideways. The abominathol had never fought a man who did not cave in to its savage blows. This human who battled him growled and snarled as much as the beast-man, and his fists felt like hammers banging into its face and sides.

Man and beast-man surged to their feet and for a few seconds their arms moved like pistons as they drove fists and paws at one another, standing almost toe to toe. The terrified woman crouched beside the firestones bit her knuckles, eyes wide and frightened.

Risking death from a possible broken neck, the abominathol lowered its head and charged. Its hard skull hit Kothar in his middle, carried him backward into the hood of the chimney. He rammed that stone sheathing with his back and head, it felt as if he had been struck with a warmace.

For an instant, Kothar sagged.

In that moment, the beast-man struck. Its paws locked together and came up hard beneath the chin of this man who would not yield. Kothar went backward and hung a moment against the bricks of the chimney.

The beast-man whirled and reached for Ahrima. Its snarl made its ugly face even more hideous, and the blood running from its lips and nose added to the ferocity of its appearance. Its huge paws caught up the shrinking woman, hoisted her over a shoulder.

It leaped for the broken opening in the side of the hut.

Kothar stood with his back propped against the chimney bricks, dragging in great gulps of air. He was growling in his throat, telling himself he ought to let the abominathol run off with Ahrima. Let the beast-man kill and eat the demon-wench, if he wanted, or add her to his harem. He would be rid of her and—

It was not Ahrima, but Mahla who was being taken, he remembered. Little golden Mahla with the sweet smile, whose spirit wandered eternally in cold, grey Nifferheim.

With a bellow, Kothar leaped.

He sprang onto the back of the beast-man, his arms slid under his armpits. Behind the abominathol's broad neck he locked his giant hands.

The beast-man staggered, dropping the woman.

The weight of the barbarian atop his back would not have impeded the massive abominathol, ordinarily. But the steel-thewed arms and hands were bending his head forward, and the massively muscled thighs and calves had a grip on his middle that squeezed his insides into a knot.

It could not reach those tightening legs to pry them apart because its arms were held out at right angles to its body by the arms beneath his armpits. And the pressure on its neck was growing more deadly by the moment. Kothar grunted, applying more of that awful pressure. The beast-man sobbed, gasping for breath, unable to do more than stand helplessly, being bent forward with inexorable force.

It ran forward suddenly, hoping to slam into the hut wall and dislodge its leechlike attacker. At the last moment, the Cumberian turned it so the top of its skull slammed into the wooden plankings.

It was not a hard blow but it seemed to rouse the beast-man to a fury of madness. Its thick lips slavered with froth, its eyes rolled in its skull, it tried to scream but could make only a mewling sound.

Furry white legs carried it back and forth at the dead run across the room. Ahrima had shrunk against the chimney bricks, eyes wide, the back of her hand to her open mouth. She knew the animal might of the abominathol, she could not believe that a mere man—even such a physical giant as Kothar—could be killing the beast-man even though she was seeing it done before her eyes.

The thing was bent double, now, like an old man crippled with age. Kothar rode its bowed back like some ghastly parasite, sapping its strength. Its red-rimmed milky eyes rolled as it sighted the girl framed against the hearth bricks. It began to stumble toward her.

By turning itself sideways, it might catch her soft throat in one of its paws and throttle the life from her. Kothar was aware of this; he roared at Ahrima.

"Out of the way! Out of the way!!"

Ahrima could not move, she stood frozen in mingled fascination and fear. Having put on human flesh, she was helpless against the human emotions that flooded her demon spirit.

Kothar growled and applied even more pressure with his arms. His muscles bulged until his sun-bronzed flesh appeared bloated to the point of splitting. The beast-man tried to scream but made only a gurgling sound in its throat. Its legs began to quiver.

Its furry paw touched Ahrima; fell away.

The abominathol sagged toward the floor. Kothar whirled it, drove its skull hard into the chimney bricks. There was a sodden sound, blood appeared on the white fur covering its poll.

As it dropped, Kothar put out one final effort.

kraaa-aaakkk

The beast-man went limp, its neck broken.

Over its dead body, the barbarian grinned up at the woman. "You're safe enough now," he rumbled.

Her breasts quivered as Ahrima fought for breath. Her eyes were glazed with the experience she had suffered. Her palms were wet, her heart was exploding in her chest. Three times she licked her lips with her tongue before she could speak.

"By the gods of Bandamarr! Man, you please me!"

Kothar let his eyes blaze at her. "Enough to win your help against Red Lori?"

She paused, tightening her fingers against the chimney bricks where she leaned, nodding her head until the long yellow hair that reached to her waist made rippling movements. "Yes—yes, but not now. I am under vow to her. I cannot break my promise. Ah, but when she is free—perhaps then I can help you, Kothar!"

"And in return for that help?"

She shook her head. "I do not know, yet. I find that being human has its own rewards. Fright. Pleasure—in seeing a man fight for you." Her hand made a waving motion in the air. "The smell of food cooking, the cold air, the sensation of touch, are all things I know nothing of, in the world out of which I came."

She watched him rise, catch hold of the dead body. "What are you doing with that thing?"

"Putting it outside, where it will freeze stiff against the broken wall planks. It will get colder, much colder before morning, and the mountain winds will try to get in here at us. The abominathol made that opening, let him block it."

When he returned, Kothar built up the fire, and taking the steaks off their steel hooks, handed one to the woman.

"Eat," he told her. "You'll need a full belly to keep you warm against the coldness."

She watched him sink his big white fangs in the juicy meat. With a sigh, she followed his example and found the steak to be delicious. The kavv he poured into two earthenware cups was sweet and warming. To her surprise, Ahrima decided she was very comfortable.

Only when Kothar shook out the two saddle blankets, handing her one, did she refuse. "These things stink of horseflesh. I couldn't."

The man stared at her, shrugged, and wrapped both blankets about himself. He lay down close to the fire. Outside the hut the wind wailed and snow blew in antic flurries. Ahrima wrapped her arms about herself, sitting huddled over on a low stool, trying to absorb the last bit of heat from the flames.

After a while, Kothar threw back a corner of the blanket. "Get in here," he said gruffly. "You'll freeze almost as solid as the abominathol, sitting there. My body heat will warm you."

Ahrima offered no objections. She dropped, wriggled herself against him, and let him throw the horse blankets over them. In moments, she was warmer, more comfortable.

Sleepily, she threw an arm about him, hugging him.

Kothar muttered, "Sleep, Ahrima. Mahla is like a baby sister to me—and you wear her body."

The she-demon smiled lazily. "Another time, Kothar," she promised, and began to laugh, softly and with promise in her throat.

5

Commoral City was asleep, though the noonday sun hung high overhead and its streets were filled with men and women. Everywhere that Kothar looked, he saw faces and bodies frozen in the middle of a movement, eyes wide and staring, lips parted while frozen in mid-speech. Marveling, he walked Greyling onward, holding the reins of the white mare.

Ahead of him walked Ahrima.

Her body was clothed in a shimmering blue cloud out of which little lightnings stabbed. She had dismounted just outside the city gates which were wide open to permit farm carts and wagons to bring produce into Commoral City.

"It is time now to use my demoniac powers," she had told him.

Her hands had stripped down her garments even as that blue cloud formed about her flesh. Instantly, the clangor of a smith's hammer on white-hot metal ceased, there was no more talk. The heavy strides of a gate guard halted, the creak of wooden hubs and axles ceased to be.

Everywhere, men and women paused in their everyday affairs, under the spell of this wizardry. Ahrima walked forward through the gate, and Kothar had no choice but to follow her.

In front of them stood the glistening stone bulk of

the palace, and to one side, the graceful lines of the Audience Hall, in which Queen Elfa of Commoral held court and distributed justice to her people. From the wooden rafters in the high-vaulted ceiling of that Audience Hall, two cages hung.

In the golden cage was imprisoned the fallen king, Markoth.

In a silver cage sat the witch-woman, Red Lori.

Kothar grinned, remembering how he had helped the wizard Kazazael defeat the Lord Markoth, how he had stopped Red Lori from completing the incantations that might have destroyed Kazazael. Queen Elfa had hung them both in cages here, as reminders to other possible recalcitrants of the fate suffered by those who opposed her royal will.

In front of the door of the Audience Hall, Ahrima paused.

Kothar swung down, went up the marble steps and gripped the door-pull rings, tugging on them. The bronze gates swung outward, and the barbarian walked into the huge Audience Hall.

"Welcome, Kothar!" cried a voice.

He looked up at the silver cage and the naked woman in it. For many months Red Lori had sat behind these pale, glittering bars, helpless. Now the time of her deliverance was at hand.

"Ahhh—and Ahrima the friendly demon!" Lori mocked.

Ahrima said in a cold voice, "I have obeyed you, Lori. I have brought the man, I hold the city under spell that he may do his work."

Kothar studied the silver cage, noting its inaccessibility. He growled, "I'll need a long rope, an iron hook."

"In the door beyond the transept, barbarian," called Lori, "you will find such a hook and such a rope. It is how they feed me, by sending up baskets of food."

He found the hook with a pulley attached just below it and a long rope by which her jailers could send little baskets up to the cages, fastened to loops set here and there in the rope. He lifted them and carried them back to the hall.

He twirled the hook, sent it flying high. It missed the first time but on his second try, the barbed end sank into the cage floor. The barbarian gathered the two dangling rope lengths in his hands and began mounting.

Like a monkey, he scrambled upward until he could put a hand on a silver bar. He dragged himself upward, setting his feet between the bars and on the bottom of the cage. Red Lori stood now, watching him with her slanted green eyes in which hope warred with mockery.

His huge hands fastened about the silver bars. There were thaumaturgic signs and sigils on those bars but they were there to prevent sorcery from harming them, they were useless against the huge muscles of the youthful giant who clung to them. Those muscles bulged, the bars began to bend.

Red Lori laughed softly, "Only you could do it, Kothar!"

He widened the space between those bars and watched as the witch-woman ducked between them and pressed herself against him.

"Hold me, barbarian. Carry me to safety!"

"I could drop you," he snarled. "I ought to drop you. There's no magic in you now, Kazazael removed all that. You're just a woman."

Anger touched her face, mingled with fear. "Ahrima would blast you!" she retorted.

"I'm not so sure," he grinned. "She might be happier if you were out of the way, Red Lori. It would give her a freer hand."

Her eyes widened, close to his. "So? You've put

some sort of male spell on her? Have you made love to her, barbarian?"

"Not while she wears the body of Mahla, no."

"Then carry me!"

His arm slipped about her middle, he lowered himself gingerly until the cage floor was level with his eyes. His legs and feet twisted into the ropes below him. Then he let go his grip and stabbed fingers at the ropes.

Using the pulley, he lowered himself and his companion to the floor below. When his feet touched the stone flaggings, he released her.

Red Lori turned to the woman. "My thanks, Ahrima. I am in your debt."

The girl who was Mahla merely inclined her head.

"Come," the witch-woman ordered. "The spell has lasted a long time. We must ride, now—before the people wake."

They made good time through the silent city streets. At a market stall, Red Lori hurriedly selected garments to cover her nudity, and a fur cloak to throw about her shoulders. Ahrima, still surrounded by her necromantic blue cloud out of which the golden lightnings spurted, had gone on ahead, since she was on foot.

Beyond the city gates, Ahrima halted. Slowly the blue clouds faded until she too, was as unclothed as Red Lori had been.

Ahrima gasped and bent her slim white legs, trying to cover her nudity by stooping forward and using her arms and her hands. "Mizran help me," she cried.

Kothar swung around, and grinned. The female demon had gone back to her own world; instantly, the spirit of Mahla had returned from Nifferheim to occupy her own true body. Mahla lacked the bold lewdness of Ahrima, she was dying of embarrassment and fright, finding herself naked outside the gates of Commoral City.

He tossed a cloak to her. "Cover yourself," he grunted.

She did as he bid, turning her head to study the great gate of Commoral City and Red Lori where she sat the saddle of the white mare. Tears were forming in her eyes and she began to sob.

"You know me, Mahla," Kothar said gently.

"I do? Oh yes. You're—Kothar."

"Your father sent me to rescue you from the worshipers of the dark god. You didn't know that, nor that a demon spirit has been inside your body while your spirit wandered in Nifferheim."

"It was awful," she whimpered.

His hand reached down to clasp hers as he kicked a fur-flapped warboot free of the iron stirrup. "Mount behind me, girl. We've a long way to go."

"To Memphor," Red Lori said coldly.

"To Clon Mell, first. I return Mahla to her father."

Red Lori sat up straighter as if to argue, but Kothar was toeing Greyling to the gallop. "The city is waking, witch-woman. Stay there—and be recaptured!"

She kicked the mare into a run.

All that long day, Red Lori was silent, galloping behind him, but Kothar knew her mind was alive, planning what was to come. He paid her little heed, he was too interested in soothing the fears of Mahla.

"It was a dead place," she told him, arms clasped about his middle and seated on the croup of the big warhorse. "All rock and grey gravel. The sky was as grey as the stones, and there was no place to go, all I could do was wander here and there and never see another living thing."

"You're safe out of the place. Forget it!"

"How can I forget it? When I close my eyes, I see it—and me in it. I shall never be able to forget it."

"In time you will."

Her arms tightened about his lean middle and he felt the weight of her head on his back. "With your help, I could," she breathed, and fell asleep.

Kothar slowed his headlong gallop so that she might sleep in some semblance of comfort. Within seconds, Red Lori was at his side, face flushed, eyes blazing.

"Go faster," she cried. "Don't you realize they'll have discovered that I'm not in my cage any longer and that Queen Elfa will have riders out scouring the city and the countryside for me? You know what she will do if she recaptures me!" She added slyly, "And to you, as well!"

"Use your witch tricks to stop her," he grumbled.

"You know I cannot!" she flared. "My magic is gone, taken from me by Kazazael! I'm just an ordinary woman, now."

He showed his teeth in a mirthless grin. "Maybe I ought to stick a dagger between your ribs and leave you for dead. Then I'd be free of you forever."

Her taunting laughter rang in his ears. "What? And have Ahrima return to displace Mahla's spirit once again? Next time, she might not release her body so easily, Kothar. She has taken a fancy to you, barbarian."

There was enough truth in what the witch-woman said to worry him, Kothar admitted to himself. He dared not take the risk. He must find a better way to rid himself of the sorceress. He wondered what it was she wanted in Memphor.

At a steady canter they rode through the flatlands of Commoral, but instead of crossing the mountain pass between Commoral and Gwyn Caer, he angled Greyling southward, to go around those high hills. His first duty was to return Mahla to her father. Afterward, he could concern himself with the witch-woman.

They rode into Clon Mell with the rising sun, mingling with the artisans and the craftsmen of the city on their way to their shops and stalls. The smell of freshly grown vegetables and newly made cheeses and bread filled the air at this early hour. Clon Mell was a great trade city, where hungry travelers from as far eastward as Makkadonia and from the southerly corners of Vandacia and Abathor came with wine and leather goods and fine horses to sell for good gold pieces in the many marts of the city.

Red Lori hung back a little, saying, "Go with the girl to her father. I shall wait for you in the street of the booksellers, where there is a thing I want to purchase."

Kothar cocked an eyebrow at her. "And what shall you use for money? The merchants of Clon Mell do not trade for smiles from pretty girls."

"You shall pay," she nodded sweetly, "from the reward monies old Pahk Mah will pay you for having rescued his daughter."

Kothar shrugged and rode on.

His knock on the locked door of the shop brought Pahk Mah hurrying to unbolt it. Father and daughter fell into an embrace while Kothar shifted uncomfortably from foot to foot.

Then the old man lifted his tear-wet eyes to study the barbarian. "What can I give you, Kothar—to pay you for what you've done?"

"Fair exchange for my jewels. No more."

"I shall add a bonus," Pahk Mah nodded, "though it shall bankrupt me. I am a loving father, you understand, and not one to show ingratitude."

"You're an old fraud, Pahk Mah. Just give me honest value."

"In what way?"

"Pay me in silver bars."

The old man stared. "In silver? You'll need a horse to carry the weight."

"Then add the horse, and a sack of coins."

"Good silver I have, from Phalkar. Bars of the finest metal, each one stamped with the Phalkarian leopards. The bars will not need to be so heavy, because the silver itself will be purer, though you'll still need a mount to carry them."

"And saddlebags to hold them," Kothar nodded.

The old man led the way between suits of lacquered armor from distant Mongrolia, past tables heavy with porcelain masterpieces and cases of rare coins. His shop was a little sampling of the world he lived in, Kothar thought, remembering the horn bow and how it had served him. His hand brushed over the jeweled surface of a golden mask placed face up on the long wooden counter.

"I ride to Memphor in Aegypton," he said casually, as Pahk Mah made marks on a length of scroll with a quill pen.

"Into the land of tombs and crypts," the old man nodded. "A dusty land, that's Aegypton. What seek you there?"

"Service with the Pharah. I'm a soldier by trade, and I've been a wanderer too long."

"Beware the tombs, they hold ghosts," Pahk Mah grinned, straightening and pushing the scroll so Kothar could read his figures.

In minutes, two young helpers came to fetch silver bars from the basement storerooms, gleaming lengths of greyish metal that glittered where the sunbeams touched them. Kothar nodded at sight of them, and turned to Pahk Mah.

"Where's Ishral?"

"They found him dead by the Thistern Abbey ruins," Pahk Mah snarled. "I think it was he who arranged to have my girl slain in the dark rites—for a promise from the high priest that he would be made youthful once more and be given his manhood back by Pulthoom."

The metal bars filled six big leather saddlebags. The young helpers led out a roan horse and tossed the bags over a blanket resting on its back, fastening them with wires. One of them led the horse forward by a rope bridle and matching reins.

Pahk Mah handed the barbarian two bags heavy with coins.

"Go with Mizran," he murmured.

Mahla came to kiss his cheek, her blue eyes veiled in shyness. "Come again soon, Kothar. I will pray for you, every night as long as I live. You cannot guess what it was you rescued me from."

Then he was mounting up on Greyling, urging the big warhorse toward the street of booksellers. His keen eyes picked out Red Lori in her red wool cloak, standing patiently beside the white mare. She carried a small rope bag in which Kothar made out several books.

"A dozen golden dikkars," she stated.

Kothar blinked. "A dozen dikkars? It's a fortune! What sort of books did you buy?"

"Books that shall aid me in my tasks. Pay the shopkeeper."

Grumbling, the barbarian did as she bid, marveling how the words of Afgorkon always came true. No matter how much of a fortune he amassed, he could never keep it so long as he carried the sword Frostfire. When he was done, he saw that Red Lori was seated on the white mare, turning it to ride out of Clon Mell.

Seconds later, he was following her, leading the roan by its rope reins. He wondered if he were riding to his death.

They went by way of the southern passes into the lands of the baron lords, along the eastern slopes of the tall mountains known as the Roof of the World, skirting the fringe of the Haunted Lands. Their camps were lonely fires at the base of a snow-tipped mountain, or on an island in the middle of the great swamps.

At every camp, Red Lori went away from him to sit on a rock or a stretch of flat ground, cross-legged, to open her books and study them. She sat there with bent head, brows furrowed in concentration, while he cut the meat for their stews or hung meat chunks over the flames on a bent stick and a thin wire.

He noticed too, that there were maps in the books, which she spread out and stared at for long periods of time, as if she memorized their lines. Besides the maps, bits of parchment rustled as she opened them, and these too, she appeared to memorize.

He had to call her several times before she would hear him and come to eat, walking dreamily and with her eyes gazing blankly. At these times, he thought she was not so much the witch-woman as a lonely, frightened girl. He grew aware that Red Lori was groping for something lost to her.

Red Lori had forgotten her hate for him, and her determination for revenge, or so it seemed. During the days she rode quietly behind him, in his shadow. At their nighttime meals, she stirred to soft laughter after she had eaten, and told him tales of her past enchantments. She was a learned sorceress, she had come close to destroying mighty Kazazael, long ago. It was only by his own efforts that she had been overcome.

Yet now she seemed to have forgotten her desire for revenge.

Kothar could not understand it.

They left the swamplands for the long steppes that began the homelands of the Mongrolians, fierce nomad riders who raided and looted wherever there was a chance at profit. Kothar was wary of these horse-archers, he would have preferred to go over the Roof of the World, but Red Lori would have none of it.

"It would take too long," she pointed out. "And I am in a hurry. I am helpless, the way I am—and I do not like to be helpless."

Her slanted green eyes studied him across the campfire. "I need a bodyguard like you, Kothar. Someone who must obey me, yet a man who can fight demons if need be."

"Where are we going?" he asked bluntly.

"To Memphor."

"But why? What's in Memphor that's so important?"

"Secrets I must master, to become as I was."

He grinned, reaching for another slab of meat. "And then? What happens to me when you're a sorceress again?"

"I haven't decided," she murmured, brooding at him, chin on fist. "I hate you, you know that. I am determined to have my vengeance on you, but I haven't made up my mind yet just what direction that revenge will take."

"I ought to lose you, maybe choke the life out of you or run my swordblade through your middle."

"You won't. Ahrima will re-possess little Mahla— and you're too tender-hearted to see the girl suffer. It's amazing, really. A big clod of a barbarian like you, nursing sentimental feelings toward a girl who doesn't mean a thing to you."

She shook her head and laughed, and on that note their talk ended. She went back to her maps and her books, reading by the firelight, while he rubbed down their horses and cleaned the wooden platters and cups of the debris from their meal.

On the sixth day after leaving Commoral City, Kothar sighted a long line of men and animals moving across the vast prairie. He stood in the iron stirrups and let his gaze assess that length of moving life.

"A caravan," he said after a time. "I thought at first it might be Mongrols, but it's moving too slowly."

"We'll join them," she told him.

"They seem to be moving toward the southwest, and Memphor lies in that direction. They'll have hired mercenaries to protect them against Mongrol raids. It might be a good idea."

They toed their mounts to a gallop.

An hour before the sun set, they pulled up before a bearded trader out of Makkadonia, who listened to their invented tale of two wanderers who had lost their way. As he quoted a price, he tugged at his beard and studied the horizon.

"Ten gold pieces each," he said.

Kothar snorted. "Ten gold pieces? You ought to pay me for riding with you. If the Mongrols attack—"

The merchant whipped around, jabbing a finger at the barbarian. "If the Mongrols attack, you and your woman will be glad to have my soldiers here, to protect you both. Now the price is twenty gold pieces, pay or leave."

He paid, at Red Lori's urging.

They were assigned a place in the line toward the rear. A big wagon filled with linen and silk goods from Athenos made a soft bed for Red Lori. Kothar himself would sleep on the ground beneath the wagon, wrapped in his saddle blankets. Paying out good gold for such dubious protection—Kothar would rather have trusted to himself and Frostfire against an enemy than the overfat mercenaries in steel caps and chainmail who served the caravan—was a waste of good gold.

The only thing he got out of it, the Cumberian decided, was that he did not have to get up during the night to put more wood on the campfires. The guards did this, so that the travelers could get an unbroken rest.

For two days, Kothar and Red Lori rode with the caravan.

On the morning of the fourth day, the Mongrols struck.

6

They came riding out of the early mists that shrouded the ground in billowing white fog, like the fabled ghosts of Jagthanoy, shaking their wooden bows above their fur-flapped caps but uttering no sound. Only a faint thunder that ran along the ground told the guards that anyone but themselves were abroad on this vast flatland, and the guards were too sleepy to notice.

The vibration woke the barbarian.

Instantly he was awake, rising upward and tossing the saddle blankets aside. He had heard the drum of hooves galloping, often before. He reached for his swordbelt, bellowing.

"Hoy—the guards! Hoy! Raiders coming!"

He snatched at his horn bow and quiver of arrows in the middle of a run for the wagon. A man was rubbing sleep from his eyes, blinking, off to one side. Kothar caught him by the shoulders, whirled him sideways so that he fell away from a wagonwheel he had been using as a prop and sprawled full length on the ground.

"Red Lori," he roared, lifting a strip of canvas.

She was sitting upright, clutching a robe to her shoulders. Her green eyes were enormous. "What is it?"

"Raiders, probably Mongrols! They're devils. They ride like the wind and shoot like Parphian who was chief archer to King Brabinak the Wise, centuries ago in Cumberia. Stir your carcass, girl! Up!"

Her hands dropped the fur robe, grabbed for blouse and woolen skirt. The quick fear that ran in her turned her cheeks an ashen hue. She dressed with her eyes on the big Cumberian as he strung his bow and loosened the arrows in the quiver that he carried over a shoulder by its leather thong.

"Are there many of them?" she breathed.

"Too many," he rasped. "Listen!"

Even she could pick out that thunder now, and interpret it. The guards were running here and there, brandishing their weapons. Their leader, a corpulent Makkadonian, was hastily buckling on his armor and shouting commands to which nobody listened. Everywhere, women were screaming and men shouted where only the wind listened.

Kothar grabbed her arm, helped Red Lori from the wagon. "We'll make a run for it," he told her. "Our horses are rested, they haven't been extended by the slow caravan pace of the last few days."

"Are you mad?" she sobbed. "Leave the caravan's protection? Put our trust in horses? You run, if you want. I stay!"

His hand called her attention to a pair of guards running past them. Kothar sneered, "Would you trust in such as those? They're soft, flabby. What muscles they ever had, have turned to mush!"

"Nevertheless, I stay!" She twisted her arm free of his grip, panting and staring up into his face with angry eyes.

He grinned coldly, gesturing to the west. "Too late to run, anyhow. See there, where another line rides out of the rising sun." He sighed and began lifting arrows out of the quiver, digging them into the ground at his feet, point first. "Ah, well. I always knew I'd die in battle. Get behind me, girl. My body will protect yours."

"If you hadn't put me in that cage," she berated his

broad back as he shoved her behind him, "I'd be able to overcome them with a spell, or whisk us off to a pleasure boat on the Outer Sea! But now I'm trapped without my wizardries. Kothar—I could kill you!"

He grunted, "Pray to your gods, Lori—that you're still alive by nightfall and me with you." He was done with his task, and studied the twenty arrows jutting their feathered shafts upward into the air. "Tell you what. If you still live by nightfall and I've saved you— call off your vendetta against me."

She ignored him to shade her eyes and watch the Mongrols gallop closer. They were short, swarthy men, heavily muscled, in chainmail shirts and woolen jerkins. Each man had learned to ride a shaggy steppes pony and wield the bow that would be his main weapon as a horse-archer, from infancy. They were reputed to be the finest cavalry in the world; each man was a separate fighting unit in himself.

The fur-flaps of their brocade caps jounced as they toed their ponies to the gallop. They came on like the kelets, the evil demons who were worshiped by the Mongrol tribes, screeching and yelling. A bow twanged. Kothar watched the flight of the arrow, dark against the sky, as it curved up and away.

"Brace yourself," he growled. "They ride right at the wagons, change direction, hit the wagons at a slant. They kill, they hurl blazing torches, they spread fear and panic."

Of its own accord, her hand went out to touch the fur jerkin that he wore under his own mail shirt. The contact sent a stab of reassurance through her. Red Lori said, "Save me, Kothar—and our feud is forgotten!"

"Your feud, not mine," he snarled.

His bow lifted, an arrow nocked to the string. No sense wasting shafts, he only had a score of them, but he would be ready if the Mongrols changed direction and came at their end of the caravan.

Up ahead, the mercenaries were firing their own bows.

"Fools," Kothar growled. "They waste their shafts."

The shafts fell far short. And then the galloping archers were within range and the air filled with their arrows. Men screamed as those points went into them. Here and there, the shrill cry of a woman told where a misdirected shaft had found softer flesh. It was not the custom of the Mongrols to slay the women, they wanted them for slaves.

Kothar waited until the horse-archers were less than one hundred yards away. Then he bent the horn bow, felt it quiver as he released his arrow. His eyes followed its course until it sank into the chest of a rider. As the rider slid from his kak, the Cumberian was already firing his second shaft.

For long minutes, the barbarian shot and shot, until his arrows had dwindled in number to five. All around him the caravan was in a wild melee. Guards were down, dying. Merchants were running about from wagon to wagon as if seeking a way out of this trap the Mongrols were drawing about them.

The clang of steel on steel could be heard where the Mongrols were using their curving scimitars against the straight steel blades of the caravan guards. Fires had sprung up, red flames and black smoke rising toward the immensity of blue sky above the prairie.

Red Lori was sobbing, gnawing on her knuckles. Her frightened eyes went from a man dragging himself along the ground and dripping blood as the arrow in his side let out his life, to a woman clinging to her baby and on her knees as if to beg pity of the horsemen. To Red Lori's anguished stares, only the barbarian seemed calm, unmoved.

For every arrow Kothar had shot, a Mongrol had died. Their bodies lay on the plain beyond the wagons. Other than those dead, the vast steppes seemed curiously empty.

A rider loomed up, scimitar in hand. His face was split by a big grin as he aimed his steel at the giant bulk of the Cumberian. Kothar grunted, sent his last arrow upward into the man.

His hand yanked at his sword, ripped Frostfire free of the scabbard. He leaped for the riderless horse, using the dead body as a mounting block to fling himself upward into the high-peaked saddle.

"Come on, girl!" he bellowed. "This is our chance!"

She ran to him, was caught by the wrist and swept upward, to land with a thud on the croup of the shaggy plains pony. The horse whinnied its disapproval of this double weight but the heels drumming its sides sent it into a headlong gallop.

Head down, Red Lori bent behind Kothar, clinging to his middle with her arms. Kothar raced away from the blazing wagons and dying men, the women who were already being stripped for the raping. Soft outlanders! he thought. With a score of Cumberians, I could have destroyed those archers. They would not have panicked as the mercenaries had done, they would have made their arrows count.

They rode in a blacklash of sound from the burning wagons. The Mongrols were off their horses and moving here and there, hunting out wounded men and slaying them, dragging merchants from under wagons to run them through with already bloody steel. The women were wailing, they were seeing their babies and children slain before their bulging eyes.

The Mongrols would kill the older women, Kothar knew, or those unattractive enough to serve as body slaves. They might even save a few women for the torturing later at night when they made camp. The torturing would rouse their lusts, they would begin arguing over the females, then, in the heat of aroused senses.

He rode into the south, into an unexplored region that included the upper reaches of Vandacia and Abathor, where few men ever ventured. It was said by some to be haunted by ghosts and demons, but Kothar would rather take his chances with those than with the horse-archers. His heels banged the pony's side, making it run even faster.

"My books," cried Red Lori suddenly. "My precious maps!"

"Are they more precious than your life?"

"Almost! Turn back, Kothar!"

His laughter was harsh upon the wind. From time to time he turned his neck, studying their back trail. No pursuit had been mounted as yet; their flight might even gone unobserved. Kothar told himself this luck could not last. They would be seen and followed. The Mongrols never relaxed their hold on a man or a woman unless death came to claim him.

Yet it seemed they might make it.

The caravan wagons were low on the horizon, the black smoke rose upward at a greater distance. The Mongrols would be too busy looting and raping to bother about a pony carrying off a man and a women, he hoped.

He set his face to the prairie in front of him, eyes ranging that wide expanse of tall grass and small rocks, hunting for a possible hiding place. There was none, he could see that at a glance; yet he went on hoping.

"Kothar!" Red Lori screamed. "They come!"

There were thirty of them, far behind them but gaining at every step. They rode bent forward in their kaks, hard of face and merciless. Their bows were on their backs, they were more intent on overtaking their quarry than in overcoming him.

Their pony stumbled under them.

In another moment, it would fall. Kothar cursed.

7

Even his great strength could not keep the pony upright for very long. Its legs were wobbling, its tossing head hurled globs of saliva from its foam-flecked lips; behind them, the Mongrols were closing in fast. Already, there were arrows whistling through the air.

Pain dug into Kothar's shoulder, into his thigh. With a hoarse cry of rage he kicked his feet free of the stirrups, threw a warbooted leg over the pony's head and slipped to the ground.

"Ride on, girl!" he bellowed.

Frostfire was in his hand, it rose to deflect a shaft and then another. The Mongrols were all around him by this time; his blade flailed sideways and to the right. The arrow shafts protruding from thigh and shoulder hampered his movements, but there was nothing wrong with his sword arm and his right leg.

Blood flecked the blue steel as it slashed through mail and flesh. A rider dropped, right arm gone at the elbow, another fell back with his chest dripping redly. The wail of a third nomad gurgled into nothingness as the barbarian yanked his blade from a throat.

He did not see Red Lori, he did not know whether she had won freedom or not, he was too concerned with trying to save his own skin. The odds were fearful but he had fought and won against fearful odds at other times. Savage blood beat in his veins, a battle rage shook him, he was snarling and cursing, sobbing air into his lungs and panting as he sprang from one place to the next, plying his steel with unstoppable fury.

Six men were down on the ground, three more sat their saddles wounded. The Mongrols were cursing now, using their curving scimitars like whips, trying to get at him.

A blade slashed his arm even as its wielder died. A second sword came in, and Kothar was slow in making his parry. There was a ring of steel on steel and he caught a blur of motion to one side of his head. Then the sword hit and—

He lay for hours among the dead.

Overhead the vultures wheeled and dipped, waiting. There were eight bodies on the ground, all of those bodies were dead but one. In a little while, all eight men would be in the spirit world.

The living man stirred. He groaned. His arm lifted and fell. After a time he pushed himself upward to his knees. His face stared up at the sky where the black birds flew, and a snarl rumbled in his thick throat.

"Damned scavengers," he growled, and sought to rise.

He stared down at his left thigh when his leg would not support his weight. A broken arrowshaft bobbed there to his movements. He put a hand to the shaft, worked it gently back and forth. Pain bit his flesh and ran all through his body, but he persisted. After a time, the point came out.

He threw it aside, scooped a handful of dirt and pressed it to the wound. The dirt would help to clot the blood. It was an old trick he had learned from a mercenary in the Foreign Guard of Queen Elfa.

Kothar could stand now. He put his hand to his head, his palm came away wet. The swordstroke which he remembered only dimly had done this. Luckily,

Frostfire had turned to the edge so that only the flat of the blade had struck him. He would live, even if his head ached for a while.

A more serious thing was the arrow in his shoulder. He could get his fingers on it but he could not work it out. If it remained in his flesh, it might fester and then, surely, he would die. Kothar snarled, staring around the grassy plain.

He must find a rock. He could lie down and rub the shaft against the rock, and perhaps dislodge it in that manner. It would hurt, but he was used to hurt. The hurt would go away after a time, and he would be alive.

Finding Frostfire half-hidden beneath a corpse, he cleaned the blade and sheathed it. Hunkered down, he studied the dead bodies, noting the leather purses at their sides that held food, the nomad leather bottles containing wine or water. Kothar grinned. He was not ashamed to rob the dead, especially dead enemies.

Laden down with money, food and water, he began his trek.

After two hours, he found he was weaker than he had thought. The loss of blood was making him stumble. It even made him see visions.

There was a horse out here, a brown Abathoran stallion. It stood a hundred yards away, the wind ruffling its mane and the tasseled braidwork of its reins. It posed with proud awareness of its strength, and once in a while it shook its head.

Kothar whistled softly, and moved forward. To his surprise, the stallion did not bolt; it even advanced a little toward him. Kothar grinned and began to trot. So did the horse.

His hand caught the reins, his other hand went to the soft white muzzle and rubbed it. "By Dwallka, you're a horse to equal Greyling," he muttered.

His foot went into the stirrup, he swung up into the oddly shaped saddle, the cantle of which was high, reaching to the small of his back. The pommel was widely arched. Kothar frowned, vaguely recalling pictures of such a saddle seen in old history books.

He toed the horse to a canter. He must find a way to get the arrowpoint out of his flesh, and fast. Even the movements of the horse between his thighs added to his pain. He gave the animal its head; one direction might be as good as another.

An hour later, a building loomed like a black dot on the horizon. Kothar felt his spirits brighten at sight of it. He kicked the stallion into a run. He would be able to get help, there.

The closer he came to those dark, blackened stones, the more he began to realize there would be no help at all. He had stumbled onto a stone temple or shrine to some forgotten god. The broken columns towered upward toward the sky, but there were great gaps between them, and the arches and shattered walls of what had been the nave were half-covered over with moss and vines.

He reined in, close to the first line of pillars.

His eyes made out an altar inside the domed apse. Behind the altar was a hollowed-out niche in the solid stone. At sight of it, Kothar felt a cold chill ripple down his spine.

He came to the ground and walked forward, intending to put his back against a pillar and scrape out the arrow. As he turned, a voice whispered to him.

"No need for that, barbarian," the voice sang in the wind.

Kothar looked around him, tensing. He could see nothing, but he could hear mocking laughter as he put hand to his swordhilt.

"No need for steel between us. Can you kill a god?"

A faint sussuration made him turn. Where the stone had been hollowed behind and above the altar, it was filling now with—blackness. It billowed upward as from the ground itself, surging outward, with faint red lines streaming here and there in the ebon richness.

"I am Thurkaknorr, barbarian!"

Kothar waited.

The blackness sighed. "Ahhh. Have I been forgotten so soon? Have the years passed so swiftly in your world and not in mine? Is my name so unfamiliar?"

"I never heard of you," Kothar said honestly.

"No. I see as I look about me that all the world I know has changed. Where stood a city, and my temple on a hill high above it, is no more. The very dirt has covered the spires and the rooftops, hiding them from view. I remember the olden days and I long for them."

There was a silence as the wind moaned, playing between the broken columns of the ancient temple.

"Come closer, man," said the blackness.

When Kothar stood before the altar, the darkness reached outward, swept about the barbarian. There were tingles in his wounded thigh, in his head, and where the arrowshaft protruded from his shoulder. He heard a low chuckle, shrouded in that blackness.

"The Mongrols wounded you, left you for dead—as they robbed my temple of its almost forgotten treasures. We have a score to settle with them, you and I!"

It seemed that, within the ebon darkness, Kothar stared out upon vast plains of black sand and dirt, where crystal trees and bushes grew white against that blackness. so that it made a faery picture beneath a glittering crystal sky. Strange beings moved, here and there, and in the far distance, a magnificent building rose skyward.

"My world, man. Here Thurkaknorr reigns supreme."

The darkness withdrew, left Kothar standing motionless in front of the altar, aware of a sense of well-being he had never known. His wounds were healed, he stared at the clean, sun-bronzed skin of his left thigh, he touched palm to his head and found no clotted blood, no bruise. At his feet lay the arrow that had been in his shoulder.

"My thanks, god or demon or whatever you are. Aye, we owe the Mongrols much. I intend to pay back some of my debt!"

"How? By riding willy-nilly over these steppes?"

"Sooner or later I'll find them!"

"By that time, Red Lori may be dead."

Kothar felt his heart leap. "She lives?"

"Aye, she lives—as captive of the nomads. She is just one more bit of loot the Mongrols have been amassing on their raiding expedition." There was a slight pause, then Thurkaknorr added, "Why are you so set on rescuing her? I know from my gods—or fellow demons, if you will—that she feuds with you."

Kothar explained his reasons for serving Red Lori, to save the spirit of blonde Mahla. The demon-god listened quietly. When the Cumberian had finished, Thurkaknorr spoke again.

"So you say. Yet I know it is written in the books of Dythan that your fates are oddly interwoven, you and Red Lori. You must serve her because this is the way destiny would have it.

"Were she to be won by a Mongrol, she would bend him to her will, she would find a way to use her necromancies once again—and this must not be! Not yet, at any rate. No, the books of Dythan say that you alone have power to stop the witch-woman. Yet how, I do not know."

Kothar grinned. It was a warm feeling, knowing

that, it made him draw Frostfire from the scabbard and clang it back so that the metal rang.

"What shall I do then?"

"Bring her here. With her—bring the Mongrols!"

The blackness faded. Only the viuga winds inhabited the ruined temple with the big barbarian. Kothar shook himself, turned and walked toward the brown stallion. He would have preferred to ride Greyling but his own warhorse was probably a prisoner of the nomad raiders.

Under his weight, the brown stallion reared, then came down at a gallop, racing to the north as if it knew the mission ahead of it. Kothar gave the beast its reins, an inner voice told him the stallion was the gift of Thurkaknorr, and was something more than a mere animal.

The horse ran with unceasing speed, as though its muscles were not of this world, but another. Kothar did not bother to dismount, he ate the food and drank the water in the Mongrol canteens. The wind of his passing ruffled his shaggy yellow hair and the long furs on his jerkin, but Kothar sat like a stoneman, scarcely moving otherwise, thrilling to the speed of this supernal animal.

As the sun set, his keen nose smelled cooking fires.

Through the gathering darkness raced the beast, without pause or hesitation. Now Kothar could see the Mongrol campfires, red dots in the deepening night. He drew back on the reins, slowing his headlong pace. The stallion walked now, while the barbarian stood in the stirrups and scanned the camp.

It was set in a little hollow, where the earth dipped away to form a wide hollow. In front of a big tent were the women of the caravan, roped together, standing or sitting as they ate the stew and drank the mare's milk which formed the raiding fare of the nomad riders. On a stool over which a spotted hide was thrown, sat a big

Mongrol, his chest framed in mail shirt and red cloak, a peaked helmet on his head. Kothar assumed this must be the khan of the nomads.

Kothar shifted in the saddle, giving his muscles a rest against the hours-long ride. He waited patiently, being familiar with the methods of the raiders. They were about to begin the victory feasting; kettles and cauldrons hung over the flames, filling the air with the fragrance of meat and vegetables.

After the feasting would come the disposal of the treasure and the women. The nomads would enjoy their women, and get drunk. It might be best then to go down into the camp and take Red Lori away from them.

His eyes touched golden links, small coffers thick with jewels.

Yes, barbarian—that is the treasure of Thurkaknorr!

"How am I to take it?" Kothar wondered.

Leave that to me! Bring the woman—and the Mongrols.

Kothar grinned. He would be able to bring the Mongrols, all right—if he galloped down into the camp and yanked Red Lori up on his brown stallion! He could get himself killed that way, too. No, he would wait.

He waited until the feasting was done and the drinking had begun. A woman was led forward, stripped and made to walk up and down between the sitting ranks of horse-archers. A man stood up, drew his sword and caught the woman by a hand.

Another nomad rose, drew his own sword and leaped forward.

The men fought while the woman shrank back, terrified. Kothar watched with something akin to battle fury working in his veins. He was watching the custom called the mating duel, in which men fought for their females until one was wounded, or dead.

A cry came from one of the duelists, as he fell back with a slash across his swordwrist. The other man laughed, drove his blade into the ground to clean it, and reached for the woman he had won. Two men came to apply salve and bandages to the wounded man.

Three women were taken from the ropes and claimed by nomads before Red Lori was led forward. She stood proudly and unafraid, as though she scorned these men, but Kothar who knew her realized fear ate in her vitals.

The man on the hide-covered stool stood up, walked slowly forward. He put a hand on Red Lori and said something in the nomad tongue.

Go down, Kothar! Challenge him!

"And get myself killed?" the barbarian growled.

Even as he spoke the brown stallion was moving forward and Kothar found he was yanking Frostfire from the scabbard. His voice bugled, "I challenge, Imkak Khan! The woman is mine!"

The seated men began to rise and reach for weapons. They had posted no guards, these steppes were their home and no body of fighting men strong enough to attack them was within three hundred miles. They stared at the giant Cumberian as he rode the brown horse forward between the fireflames.

Red Lori stood proudly, her white shoulders thrown back. The man who held her long red hair twisted in a hand was glaring at the solitary rider.

While Kothar reined in his mount, Imkak Khan snapped, "You're no Mongrol, and only a Mongrol possesses the right to challenge in the mating duel."

Kothar stood before the khan, grinning coldly. "If you refuse, it proves you a coward and unfit to rule— let alone take a woman captive for your enjoyment."

He let his blue eyes roam the circle of watching nomads.

"You tried to kill me today, some of you. You left me for dead. I'm alive—and here to claim my own. Are the nomads all cowards? Don't they dare meet me in single combat? Or must they fight with odds of twenty to one to hope for victory?"

He let his mocking laughter boom out.

"You aren't men! Then what do you want with a woman?"

Red Lori smiled at him, then cried, "They are boors, Kothar. Fearful boors who are brave only when they fight with overwhelming numbers—or perhaps when they attack women."

The hand holding her hair yanked back, tugging her off balance. Red Lori cried out as she staggered. Before she could right herself, Kothar was leaping forward, his left fist swinging, ramming into the jaw of the khan.

The khan flew backward off his feet.

The nomads surged forward. Kothar snarled, swung Frostfire in front of their eyes. "Back! Before I kill you all! Is your khan a puling infant, that he cannot defend himself? Is he the kind of leader you nomads follow? Pah! I spit on him—and on you!"

The khan screamed in his fury as he came off the ground, his scimitar glinting with the firelight as he swung it. Kothar shoved Red Lori behind him, catching the fury of that steel and turning it.

The khan was a tall man, wiry in his strength. He fought like a burning flame, darting and dipping, falling to a knee and thrusting, employing overhead blows that changed in midthrust into sidewise slashes. He cursed and panted, his black eyes blazed with the battle rage.

Kothar stood like a rock, calm and scarcely moving, Frostfire turning almost of itself to ward off the blows and cuts that flew about him with blinding intensity.

Steel sang with metallic cadences, sparks flew as edge met edge.

The khan was driving Kothar back and back, to the shouted delight of his nomad riders. The barbarian let the khan turn him, because Kothar had spotted Greyling in the rope corral that held the nomads' horses. Greyling for Red Lori, the brown stallion for himself! And so he allowed the khan to turn him and he listened to the delighted howls of the horse-archers with a grim smile.

When the corral ropes touched his back and Red Lori pressed against him, Kothar made his move. He bounded away from the hemp, he slashed with Frostfire like a man freshly come into battle. His giant frame and massive muscles felt no fatigue, whereas Imkak Khan was weary from the many sword-strokes with which he had belabored the sword of the giant barbarian.

Back, went Imkak Khan. Back, until he stumbled.

The grins on the faces of his followers were gone before the scowls and glares that watched the sword-play of the Cumberian. Death for their leader glinted coldly out the blue eyes of this barbarian who watched his every move. The men sensed this, so did their khan.

"Help me!" shouted Imkak Khan.

At the same moment the great blue blade of Frostfire fell atop his skull, splitting his head from poll to chin. Blood gushed. The body of the nomad ruler swayed a moment, still on his legs—and Kothar leaped.

His arm swept Red Lori up, flung her through the air onto the bare back of Greyling, even as he vaulted the rope fence. Like a cat, the barbarian was after her, landing behind her, bloody sword flashing as he severed the corral ropes. The nomad ponies surged forward in an eruption of flying hooves and snapping teeth.

Nomad ponies are chancy beasts, at best. With the

smell of spilled blood in their nostrils, with the harsh
cries of the Cumberian ringing in their ears, they went
mad with terror. Like a tidal wave they swept from
their hempen bounds and spilled out across the camp.
They rode down their masters, trampling some, less
fleet of foot than the others, into bloody lifelessness.

Kothar and Red Lori rode Greyling through the
midst of this flash flood of horseflesh. A cry from the
barbarian brought the brown stallion galloping, using
its greater heights and weight to wedge a path between
the smaller steppes ponies.

Kothar leaped to the brown back. Greyling could
carry Red Lori. Somewhere off in the darkness, a bow
twanged. The galloping ponies had trodden down the
campfires, and the stink of singed flesh and hair was all
around them. In the darkness, the archers could not see
to shoot, yet a shaft whizzed past Red Lori, making her
cry out.

"Ride south!" Kothar yelled. "And fast!"

She bent above the neck of the grey warhorse, its
white mane stinging her cheeks, urging on the beast
with soft words and stroking hands. Fast was Greyling,
but even faster was the demon-horse between Kothar's
thighs. It raced ahead of the warhorse, its hooves barely
skimming the ground.

Behind them, order was coming out of chaos as the
Mongrols ran down their mounts and leaped on their
bare backs. Their warcry ululated to the stars as scimitars flashed and the ground shook to the thunder of
galloping hooves.

The chase went on through the hours of the night.

Long before dawn, the brown stallion and Greyling
swerved to a halt before the ruined temple. Kothar
leaped down, went to the grey horse and helped Red
Lori. She leaned against him when her feet firmed on
the ground, catching his arms and holding him.

"Let me rest a little while, Kothar. I have not your endurance. I'm exhausted. Do you have any water?"

He gave her a leather bottle and made her sip its contents slowly. The sun was rising to the east, the broken pillars of the ancient temple sent long shadows across the ground. While she sat on a plinth and got her strength back, the barbarian told her about Thur-kaknorr.

"Yes, I know the name," she murmured, "from those times when I consorted with demons during my spells and incantations. He is a very potent god, Thur-kaknorr."

"He'd better be a prompt god," the barbarian growled.

Red Lori looked where Kothar jerked his thumb. A line of dots on the northern horizon showed where the nomads came at the run. In minutes they would be upon them. She saw the barbarian glance at the hollowed stone behind the altar.

"He will come," she told him.

His answer was the sound of Frostfire scraping from the scabbard. "Useless to trust a god or demon," he snarled. "You do what they want, and one way or the other they turn on you."

He swung about, faced the north and the horse-archers, disdaining anything but the direct attack. Screeching shrilly, waving their scimitars—one or two were unfastening their bows and putting arrows to the strings—they ran on with a cloud of yellow dust rising behind them to tell the direction of their coming.

A few arrowshafts slid into the air. Two were close; these, Kothar knocked aside. Then the nomads were in front of him, and he went to meet them, swinging the blued blade, shouting the battle cry of the Cumberian Viks where he had served his apprenticeship to Dwall-ka, god of battles.

A rider went down, and another. A scimitar glanced off the barbarian's mailed shirt. Gripping a bridle, using it to support his weight, he swung from one horse to a second, driving his blade sideways into a rider and upward to disembowel a man who missed his own slash at his bared head.

"Enough, barbarian! You served to bring them close —no none may escape. Now—they belong to me!"

Every man stood frozen in horror, staring at the flat altar and the hollowed stone shell behind it, where a gathering blackness was emerging, flecked with angry red beams that pulsed and flared deep inside it. A raw fury beat outward from that ebon intelligence like a tangible thing. Even Kothar felt it lash about him.

The horse-archers were terrified. This was a king among the kelets, the evil spirits that inhabited their steppe world. Their shamans had spoken of these demons that lived somewhere in the vast wastelands over which they raced their ponies.

As one man, they screeched their fear, turned their horses to flee. But the blackness was far faster than mere flesh. It sped from the hollowed stone, raced to form twin arms on either side of the temple, extending outward.

Kothar moved steadily backward, his eyes touching Thurkaknorr and then the nomads, until his thigh met Red Lori where she sat upon the plinth, smiling dreamily.

"Watch, Kothar—and know the might of an angry Thurkaknorr!" she breathed, laughing softly and catching his hand in hers.

He was too fascinated by what was happening to shake off her hold. The nomads were galloping their ponies toward the thin line of blackness ringing them in, shouting and swinging their scimitars. One of them galloped at the thinnest section, toeing his horse for a leap.

Upward rose the shaggy steppes pony.

In the middle of their rise, a rider screamed, back arching and sword falling from his suddenly nerveless fingers. The blackness rose upward like a wall to meet him. Where his arm protruded through the blackness there was only a skeleton. The flesh had been stripped away, leaving bare bone.

"Dwallka!" bellowed Kothar.

The pony completed its leap, landing on the other side of the dark wall. Instead of a man, a skeleton sat its back, a skeleton that fell from the saddle and lay on the grassy ground—dead bones glinting in the morning sunlight.

A wail went up from the other nomads. They were going mad from superstitious terror. They glared around them, seeking a way out; there was none. They were trapped here and the blackness that was Thurkaknorr was moving slowly inward for the feasting.

You desecrated my temple! You stole my treasures! Thieves! Rapers of women! Killers of men! This day you die!

The ring closed. Men rose up in their stirrups to slash at it, but the hands that held the scimitars were bones, and the bones fell away so that only the handless wrists remained to the wildly screaming Mongrols. More men sought to ride through the blackness; they too, were turned to skeletons.

In a little while it was over. The blackness was receding into the hollowed-out stone. Shaggy ponies ran here and there, the ground was littered with human bones. Red Lori was standing, shading her eyes with an upraised hand as she stared at that which was Thurkaknorr.

And Thurkaknorr spoke.

"Go now, barbarian, with this woman. I shall recover my treasure by assembling and giving life to the bones scattered here and there, commanding them to bring me what is mine."

The blackness receded. In a moment only the stone shell itself could be seen. A steppes pony whinnied, riderless.

"Come," said Kothar.

Red Lori followed him quite meekly.

8

On Greyling, the barbarian set a fast pace toward the desert lands of Aegypton. Red Lori followed on a steppes pony. When he had looked about for the brown stallion, it was nowhere to be seen, convincing the barbarian that it had, indeed, been a creation of Thurkaknorr for his needs.

Behind them, attached to a rope rein, came the horse laden with the silver bars Pahk Mah had traded to him. Without the horse and its burden, Kothar knew he was helpless against Red Lori. He had made a special point of riding to the Mongrol encampment—where only dead men remained—to secure his horse, overriding the objections Red Lori made.

They went by lonely ways, galloping along an abandoned caravan trail, pausing on wind-swept hills to eat and sleep. Sometimes they rode without a road under their horses' hooves, the barbarian trusting to his instinct and to the sun and stars to tell him he rode south by west. At every mile they galloped, Red Lori recovered a little of her arrogance.

"I think I shall keep you alive, Kothar," she told him once when they halted to let their horses blow. "I have in mind the fact that Kazazael sent you to kill my guardians when I was too deeply involved in an incantation to help them. You make a good guardian, all by yourself."

"I belong to no one but myself," he growled.

"Oh? Is it your wish to ride with me to Memphor? Or do you come because of what might happen to Mahla?"

"Yes, because of Mahla," he answered.

"What I do now, I can do again. I can always find a way to strike at you. Remember it. Be grateful that I give you life—so serve me well."

Her taunting laughter rang out, and Kothar scowled.

They came out upon the desert sands of Aegypton seeing the grim stone pyramids rising black against the red of a setting sun. Memphor lay to the west, they could not see it from these gravel beds across which they galloped. To the south lay the forgotten ruins of Xythoron. Xythoron was a city whose eerie destruction —legends say it was by a rain of fireballs out of the dark domain of the demon-gods—lay so far in the past that none had known of its existence until a century ago, when two travelers from the land of Yurj discovered it.

There were tombs in the city ruins, strange buildings of twisted, alien architecture, of a material not known on Yarth. Only one tomb had ever been opened, by a team of diggers sent from Memphor. No man knows what came out of the tomb, only the shattered, pulpy remains of the diggers were found, as if torn apart by mad, gigantic hands. The tomb had been hastily sealed up, and today no man in his right mind walked the time-worn paving stones of cursed Xyrothon.

"There are ways to open the tombs," Red Lori hinted.

Kothar grinned, "You've lost your powers of wizardry. Won't you be taking a chance?"

"You'd like me to fail, wouldn't you?" she flared. "You'd like a demon to come out of the tomb and tear me to pieces!"

"There is some danger, then?"

"Of course there's danger—not only for me but for you as well!" She laughed shrilly. "They won't stop with me, if they're unleashed. They'll rip you limb from limb, too."

They rode on, their horses' hooves scratching sparks from the stones of the desert. Night was closing in, the sun was nothing more than a red reflection on the clouds.

"We ought to make camp," Kothar said.

"Not yet. We should be in Xythoron soon."

A coldness ran down the barbarian's spine. He had no wish to make his campfire on stones where demons walked. He preferred the clean air of mountain or steppe to the stink of embalming fluids. He did not hold with wizards and demonolotry, though he knew they existed.

His hand touched the jeweled hilt of Frostfire. There was magic in his sword, and he had the uncomfortable feeling that he might need all the magic help he could get before he got out of Xythoron alive. If he got out alive.

The stars were in the sky, clustered close together, as the first iron hoof rang on a paving-stone. Kothar walked Greyling here, uneasy at the brooding menace of the low stone buildings, their caved-in roofbeams, charred and powdery, at the marble mausoleums that rose upward between the houses. The odor of death was still in the dead air, mixed with the smells of natron and bitumen.

His hand tightened on the rope rein of the roan. He wanted the roan close, he did not intend for it to bolt and run, not when it had come so far. Red Lori rose beside him, shifting her weight in the saddle as her eyes roamed the tombs and houses. From the manner in which her eyes quested, the Cumberian knew she sought a sign to help her pick out the tomb she sought.

He waited for her to signal him.

"There," she cried, pointing. "That black tomb, with the spire. It is the crypt of the mage Kalikalides."

She swung down and ran for the bronze doors of the black mausoleum. Her hands came up, she ran palms and fingertips across the grotesque carvings and eerie imageries caught in metal by an unknown artisan. Kothar saw her nod her head as if satisfied.

He began walking into one building after another, ripping loose charred timbers and carrying out bits of wooden furniture. These he piled in the square before the tomb. Red Lori watched him, having turned away from the bronze doors, with a taunting smile on her red mouth.

"Are you making a cooking fire or a bonfire?" she asked tartly.

"Both. I don't like this place."

"Kothar the brave! Kothar the unconquerable! Like a little child, he dreads the darkness."

He grinned at her with quick humor. Lying, he said, "Yes, you might say I am afraid of the dark. The flames will keep the demons away."

"Not when I summon them up. And the fire will do you no good inside the tomb. But do what you will, I don't object."

He saw her shiver and come closer to the little flames that began licking upward at the blackened wood chips he had broken off ancient timbers with his bare hands. She was none too sure of herself and her powers, he decided. Being human at the moment, she too, had a need for warmth.

He set a stool for her beside the flames.

"What do you hope to accomplish here?" he asked as he hung a small cooking pot above the flames.

"I shall summon up Deethra. He was the mightiest

of the necromancers of Xythoron. He shall restore to me my powers."

"In exchange for what? All magicians are mammonists at heart."

Red Lori shivered, brooding down at the flames that had now reached upward to a height of five feet. Kothar watched the flames too, but he was thinking, In a few hours those charred timbers will be glowing coals, hot enough for my purpose. He looked at the witch-woman.

"When are you going to open the tomb?"

"When I have eaten. It will be a long vigil—if it is to succeed at all." Again she shivered, though the flames were hot and the wind had died down. "Deethra may oppose me, in which case—"

She raised and lowered her shoulders. "Those maps and psalteries I bought in the Street of Booksellers in Clon Mell told of the hours most favorable to the raising up of the dead age. I wish I had them with me now. I must trust to my memory or completely fail in my attempt."

"Then you'd only be a normal woman," Kothar rasped.

Her green eyes studied him. "Would you like that, barbarian?"

His hands tossed broken chair legs on the flames. "You might prove more interesting as a companion."

She rose to her feet, preening in her female pride. Her eyes touched the twin moons of Yarth moving slowly across the blue-black night sky. "There is no time to show you how companionable I might be," she murmured. "The hour of the rat is upon us, and it is time now to open the bronze gates. Come you with me, Kothar."

"Perhaps I should remain behind. Robbers, ghouls or cutpurses may be abroad."

She hooted. "In dread Xythoron? Come!"

He went with her to the gates. "Break them," she commanded.

His huge hands went to the gates, pushed inward. His muscles leaped and bulged beneath his skin. Sweatdrops touched his forehead. The bronze doors moved inward, but the iron bar that held them did not break.

Moving back a few feet, he hurled himself upon them. He heard a faint crack, but the bar still held.

As he paused, breathing heavily, Red Lori murmured, "The iron bar is very old. Very old. Even in this dry air, it must be rusted through. Try again."

A third time he hurled himself at the gates. And now they gave, so that the barbarian plummeted inward, hitting a smoothly tiled floor and rolling through a mixture of noisome, charnel odors.

"Paugh!" he said, rolling over and coming to his feet.

Red Lori came racing through the doorway, a silhouette of curves and flying hair against the starlit night. She had left the cloak on the paving-stones beside the fire, she wore only the shirt and fringed skirt of the Mongrol females, which she had donned in the nomad camp.

Kothar looked about him at the empty mausoleum. "You've ridden a fool's errand. There's nothing here."

"The floor, barbarian! Grasp that iron ring."

His eyes could make out dimly a trap door in the floor. There was an iron ring there, very rusted. Kothar bent, grasped it. His back arched; he heaved, panting. Slowly the trap door rose. As it did so, a blue light came out into the vault, illuminating it.

"Kalikalides left the light," she breathed. "It is a demon-light, that can never be extinguished. By its magic aid, his body will have the appearance of true life."

She moved to the trap-door opening, where she could see narrow steps leading downward into the crypt itself. There was a hush on the world, a silence which throbbed in the eardrums as she set first one foot and then another on those treads.

Kothar trailed her down the steps, his neck itching with supernatural dread, his hand gripping Frostfire's hilt. He did not know what he would see; the reality somewhat disappointed him.

A stone bier occupied the center of the room. On it lay a body, seemingly only recently dead, wrapped in garments of gold and purple covered with necromantic sigils. The face was flushed, as if with blood. The man's alive! Kothar thought dazedly. But no, these were the things potent magic could do, so to preserve a body.

Red Lori began to chant.

The blue lights dimmed, then glowed more brightly, but now it seemed to the Cumberian that the blue light was like mist floating in the air, flecked with tiny lights. It grew harder to see; he could not make out the body of Kalikalides quite as clearly, and even Red Lori seemed to be a long distance off.

Her chanting filled the vault, grew louder.

There was no longer a crypt about them, but a metallic room, the walls of which glowed with many colors, sending out their rays of light across the vast chamber in which he and Red Lori stood. Before them was what seemed to be a throne made out of huge metal building blocks, with a grillwork of golden tracery forming its back.

A cloud shimmered on the throne.

The cloud firmed, became the mage Kalikalides. He was the same as the dead body on the crypt slab, the barbarian saw, except that he was alive. Alive? Yes—

and no. For his eyelids were closed, though his eyes appeared to burn through their covering as he stared down on the woman and the man.

"Who wakes Kalikalides? Who dares this realm of the dead?"

"I, Red Lori. A sorceress—once. I have lost my powers. I seek them back, with your help."

"You know the rites to command my speech?"

"I do. 'By the wisdom of Asherol, by the might of—' "

"Wait!" the mage cried. "There is a mortal here, a man who knows nothing of these wizardries! Let him wait outside my realm while I do what must be done to give you back your powers."

Kothar felt those dead eyes studying him. Again that sepulchral voice boomed forth. "His presence can disturb the forces which I must summon up, which I must invest in you. He must go back."

The barbarian felt the scene blur before his eyes. He staggered a moment, then saw that he was once more inside the crypt. Red Lori was gone, the dead body of Kalikalides rested unmoving on its cold stone slab. Kothar growled a curse.

He turned and leaped for the stairs. On the upper floor, he lowered the trap door and dropped it into place. He ran for the bronze gates, slammed them together. There was no way to restore the bar that had held them closed for thousands of years, but he had a better way to seal them.

The charred timbers and the bits of furniture had burned down to red coals. The heat from those blue flames was terrible. The barbarian hoped it would be enough for his purpose.

He went to the roan, unstrapped the saddlebags. The silver bars he removed from the bags, placing them in the cooking pots he had brought along from the Mongrol camp. The cooking pots he placed on the coals.

Silver had a low melting point, he knew. He did not have to melt the silver completely, just enough so that he could work it. He labored mightily, throwing more timbers on the flames. Now he must stand by, and wait.

It was dawn when the silver was soft enough to pour from the pots. He carried those pots to the bronze gates and worked the molten silver in with his dagger, all along the cracks. When he was done, the pots were empty, but there was a solid silver seal running along the joints of the doors, and where they hung on their hinges.

Not so much as a breath of air could escape the crypt. Kothar hoped that Red Lori would be as helpless. He had gambled on the fact that Kazazael had used silver bars to contain her; no witch or sorceress could pass through anything covered with silver; something about the metal was impervious to magic.

The silver would hold her, or he was doomed.

As the sun came up, he rode out of Xythoron.

Kothar

Barbarian Swordsman

First in this series

by Gardner F. Fox

Be sure to read the first novel in the series, introducing the mightiest fantasy hero of the enchanted, terrifying world before—or beyond—recorded time.

B60-1003

60¢

FREE BOOKS!

Choose any 4 exciting Belmont Books listed below and receive the fifth book absolutely free! Choose 7 books and get 2 additional books free!

☐ **A PAIR FROM SPACE**, by James Blish and Robert Silverberg
First paperback publication of two major science fiction novels—complete.
#B92-612, 50¢

☐ **A LAMP FOR MEDUSA**, by William Tenn
THE PLAYERS OF HELL, by Dave Van Arnam
First paperback publication of Tenn's classic novel—plus a tense novel by a new
master of swords and sorcery SF. #B60-077, 60¢

☐ **ODYSSEY TO EARTHDEATH**, by Leo P. Kelley
Death is the only answer to war. #B60-085, 60¢

☐ **SPACE TUG**, by Murray Leinster
A startling science fiction novel of our country's desperate attempt to supply
our men living on the moon. #B50-846, 50¢

☐ **WHOM THE GODS WOULD SLAY**, by Ivar Jorgensen
A bold Viking adventurer was trapped in a devil's nightmare 10,000 years in
the making. #B50-849, 50¢

☐ **LORDS OF CREATION**, by Eando Binder
An immortal from the deep past dares to challenge the disintegrating future.
#B50-852, 50¢

☐ **GIANT OF WORLD'S END**, by Lin Carter
Could the combined powers of the wizard and the warrior halt the doom that
filled the skies? #B50-853, 50¢

☐ **DOOMSTAR**, by Edmond Hamilton
One man against the universe—one man with a device that could change a sun
from a life source to the ultimate death-dealing weapon. #B50-857, 50¢

☐ **KOTHAR—BARBARIAN SWORDSMAN**, by Gardner F. Fox
The mightiest fantasy hero of the enchanted, terrifying world before—or
beyond—recorded time. #B60-1003, 60¢

NON-FICTION

☐ **WORLD OF THE WEIRD**, by Brad Steiger
Startling, astounding, shocking . . . but incredibly true! A collection of stories
of human beings, and animals who defy all known laws of science and nature.
#B50-727, 50¢

☐ **FINDERS KEEPERS**, by Warren Smith
YOU can find millions in lost and buried treasure! Here are the inside tips on
how to locate money, gold and jewels for yourself! #B60-061, 60¢

☐ **FLYING SAUCERS ARE WATCHING US**, by Otto O. Binder
New evidence and startling scientific finds lead to a startling answer to the UFO
riddle. #B75-218, 75¢
